> *"I'm going to find him, Sam. I'm going to stop him, and that's not a promise, it's a guarantee."*

His certainty hung in the air. He sounded so relentlessly convinced that she actually believed him.

She tilted her head and saw his determined brown eyes, the firm set of his wide mouth, and as their gazes locked, the air in the kitchen swiftly changed. It hissed and sizzled, crackled like twigs. She wanted to look away, to walk away, to make it stop, but she stood frozen in place.

A tiny gasp tore from her throat but he covered it with his lips and swallowed it with his kiss. A gentle kiss, the soft brush of his lips against hers, the teasing flick of his tongue. The spicy, masculine scent of him infused her senses, making her woozy with desire. And yet it was a controlled kiss, one that told her he was the type of man who'd never fully let down his guard, never succumb to the pleasures of the flesh before clearing it with his head.

Dear Reader,

I'm absolutely thrilled about the release of *Silent Watch,* my debut book with Silhouette Romantic Suspense. The idea for this story came to me during a conversation with a friend, after we'd watched a news segment about the latest victim of a serial killer being found.

My friend turned to me and, very frustrated, said, "Why is it always a victim and never a survivor?"

And from that one remark, *Silent Watch* was born. I wanted to write about a heroine who had suffered at the hands of a madman, but lived to tell the tale. Not only that, but I wanted my survivor to have the strength to face the person who'd hurt her. And of course, who else to help her regain that strength but the gorgeous FBI agent assigned to protect her?

I hope you enjoy Samantha and Blake's story, and that their romance makes you believe in the healing power of love! I'd also love to hear from you. Drop me a line at www.ellekennedy.com or swing over to sizzlingpens.blogspot.com to see what some of my fellow Harlequin authors and I are blogging about.

Happy reading!

Elle Kennedy

ELLE KENNEDY

Silent Watch

Silhouette

Romantic

SUSPENSE

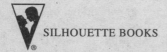 SILHOUETTE BOOKS

Recycling programs for this product may not exist in your area.

ISBN-13: 978-0-373-27644-8

SILENT WATCH

Visit Silhouette Books at www.eHarlequin.com

Printed in U.S.A.

Books by Elle Kennedy

Silhouette Romantic Suspense

Silent Watch #1574

ELLE KENNEDY

grew up in the suburbs of Toronto, Ontario, and holds a B.A. in English from York University. From an early age, she knew she wanted to be a writer, and actively began pursuing that dream when she was only a teenager. When she's not writing, she's reading. And when she's not reading, she's making music with her drummer boyfriend, oil painting, or indulging her love for board games.

Elle loves to hear from her readers. Visit her Web site www.ellekennedy.com, or stop by her blog, http://sizzlingpens.blogspot.com, to chat with Elle and fellow Harlequin writers.

I could not have written this book without the support of my family and friends, the eagle eyes of my critique partners Lori Borrill, Jennifer Lewis, Kira Sinclair and Amanda White, and the guidance of my brilliant editor, Diana Ventimiglia.

Chapter 1

Blake Corwin was about to raise a woman from the dead.

He didn't like it, and God knew if he had any viable choices left he would have left Samantha Dawson in peace and found another way to go about this. But there was no other way, no other hope except this woman who had suffered more in six months than most people suffered in a lifetime.

"She won't talk to us, you know," his partner murmured.

Blake furrowed his brows, trying to stop the frustration he felt from seeping into his expression. He adjusted the shoulder holster under his sports coat and directed a questioning look at the other man before continuing up the snowy path to the farmhouse up ahead.

"What makes you say that?" he asked, stepping over a fallen log.

"Look around you, man." Rick Scott gestured to the

isolated area. "There's a reason why she requested a safe house out of the city. No chance of any human contact."

He tried not to let their surroundings affect his sense of purpose, but he had the sneaking suspicion that Rick's assessment was accurate. Aside from the rambling white-and-green house, the land stood barren. Very few trees, grass covered by a thin layer of silver frost, and not another structure in sight. The nearest house was a mile away, and when they'd pulled into the long winding driveway earlier, Blake's chest had tightened with what he could only describe as a sense of doom.

He hated this place, hated everything it represented. Fear. Despair. Torment. The woman living here was isolated from the world, and it tore him up knowing he was partly responsible for it. A madman had put Samantha Dawson in this desolate farmhouse, but Blake's inability to catch a killer was keeping her there.

"I feel like I'm walking in a freezer." Rick shivered and pulled the zipper of his light jacket all the way to the collar. "Are you sure we're in Illinois? Seems like Antarctica."

Born and raised in Chicago, which boasted some of the coldest winters in the country, Blake merely chuckled. "Poor kid. Why don't you go back to L.A. and crawl under a palm tree?"

Rick frowned. "Don't make me pull out my gun, Agent Corwin."

"Do it. I'd love to see you explain to Knight why you shot his—and I quote—best agent."

"You're never going to let that go, are you?"

Blake offered a grin, knowing just how much it pissed Rick off. Funny, how when Blake caught a serial killer he rarely received a word of praise from Michael Knight. But when he found his supervisor's lost dog? Well, that was almost worthy of promotion.

"Who brings his dog to work anyway?" Rick grumbled. He kicked a pile of slush as he walked.

"Hey, don't look all upset. It's not my fault that Jasper was hiding in the storage room when I walked in."

Rick frowned again. "You didn't see Knight licking my boots when I brought in Butcher Betty."

"As I recall, I was there too, slapping the handcuffs on her," Blake pointed out.

Their good-natured banter died as they reached the rickety wraparound porch. A lone wicker chair sat in the corner, and hanging above the front door was a set of wind chimes that jingled cheerfully each time the cold late autumn breeze swept by. Yet there was nothing cheerful about this house, with its disheveled exterior and the layer of lime-green paint peeling and cracking on the front door.

Blake glanced around and saw that there wasn't a doorbell. Reaching out, he rapped his knuckles against the solid wood, then turned to Rick as they waited for an answer. "Think she's home?"

"She's home." Rick crooked his finger to the left. "Her car's here."

Blake couldn't believe he'd missed the pale-beige vehicle parked in the detached garage a few feet from the house. Maybe it was just the frigid November air freezing his senses. Or hell, maybe this goddamn case had finally gotten to him.

The sound of footsteps pulled his attention back to the door in front of him. His senses kicked back into place, ears perking up at what sounded like a padlock being scraped open. The clicks that followed told Blake that Samantha Dawson had not one, not two, but a total of five locks on her door, as well as a security system that beeped incessantly as the person inside deactivated it.

A fortress in a farmhouse.

Not that he blamed her for taking such precautions.

"She used to be a swimsuit model, you know," Rick remarked in a low voice.

"Well aware of that."

They stood patiently until the door opened. When it did, Blake found himself staring down the barrel of a steel-black shotgun. By instinct, he almost reached for his own gun, but when he met the eyes of the woman in front of them, he reconsidered.

She appeared more frightened than menacing. Her big gray eyes, surrounded by thick sooty eyelashes, looked so haunted that Blake's throat tightened with an emotion he couldn't quite place. He'd read her file, knew what haunted her, but somehow he hadn't expected to see the overwhelming fear lining each delicate feature of her face. And what a face it was. High cheekbones, lush pink lips, a straight aristocratic nose. In the old days men would've started wars for a woman like this.

"What do you want?" she demanded, voice deadly and gun still aimed directly at Blake's heart.

"Samantha Dawson?" he asked, though he didn't need her hesitant nod of confirmation to know who she was.

Her pictures hardly did her justice. She was a natural beauty, tall and slender, with caramel-colored hair that fell past her shoulders in waves. And damn, those eyes were mesmerizing, so gray they reminded Blake of an overcast sky. She wore jeans and a bulky blue sweatshirt.

"What do you want?" she repeated.

She didn't lower the gun, not even a fraction of an inch, and he glanced at his partner for help.

Reaching into his pocket for his ID, Rick flashed his

badge at the brunette. "Special Agent Rick Scott. The man you're pointing the gun at is my partner, Blake Corwin. We're with the FBI."

Rick's words had been meant to reassure her, but they obviously fell short of the mark. Her jaw only tightened and her shoulders stiffened as if she were gearing up for a boxing match. "Do you have a warrant to search my house?"

Caught off guard, Blake answered for his partner. "What? No."

"Are you here to arrest me?"

"Of course not," Rick said, offering a tentative smile.

Her eyes flashed. "Then I have nothing to say to you."

The door slammed in their faces so swiftly that Blake blinked in surprise. He heard the padlock scrape shut, but the fact that she didn't turn any of the other locks told him the woman was still behind the door, waiting for them to leave.

He sucked in a long breath and looked at Rick.

"Well." Rick's voice was quiet.

Feeling the onset of a headache, Blake rubbed his temples. "We can't leave. You know we can't leave without speaking to her."

Samantha Dawson was their last chance, and they both knew it. If she didn't agree to help them, the Rose Killer might slip out of their grasp and disappear into the shadows forever. How many more women would the guy murder before he was stopped? The death toll currently numbered three. Three women. Women who were somebody's daughters, somebody's wives and mothers. All gone. Except for Samantha Dawson, and of course, this latest victim.

Three dead, but two very much alive. Not a moment of mercy and compassion on the creep's part, of course; he'd left them believing they were dead. And as long as Blake and his fellow agents at the Bureau had anything to say about it, they would continue to be dead. At least until the bastard was caught and thrown behind bars.

"She's our last hope," Rick continued with a heavy sigh. "The longer Elaine Woodman stays silent, the more time this psycho has to keep killing."

The ache in Blake's temples grew stronger. It had only been three weeks since Elaine Woodman's attack, but it felt like months, especially considering that drawing information out of the young woman had been all but impossible so far. "We have no guarantee that Samantha will be able to get through to her," he said.

"But it's a chance. Elaine is too traumatized to talk about her experience, not with the shrinks, the cops, us. But another victim? Samantha Dawson has a better chance than any of us to get Elaine to open up."

Blake saw the truth in Rick's words, felt the same flickering hope that had brought him to this farmhouse, but he couldn't help but wonder if their need to catch this madman might end up hurting these surviving women.

The fear in Samantha Dawson's eyes flashed through his brain, agony he couldn't even imagine. Did they really have the right to make her experience it all over again? Sure, she'd changed her name, she was under the protection of the Bureau and hidden away in this no-horse town, but she sure as hell hadn't looked at ease when she'd opened that door.

No matter how far the Bureau had gone to keep Samantha Dawson safe, Blake knew without a doubt that she didn't feel that way.

"Come on, let's try again," Rick finally said, reaching out and knocking on her door once more.

"Get off my property," came the muffled reply.

"Miss Dawson, please—"

She cut Rick off with, "I'm holding the phone in my hands right now. I'll call the sheriff and have you charged with harassment if I don't hear the sound of your footsteps leaving my property."

"Let me talk to her," Blake said quietly.

With a nod, Rick shoved his hands into his pockets and allowed Blake to take the lead.

"Miss Dawson, you can call the sheriff if you want. Nobody's stopping you." He spoke gently, trying to offer comfort he knew she didn't feel. "I'm just asking you to listen to what we have to say before you make that call."

In response came a lengthy silence, and he'd almost given up hope when he heard the soft, "I'm listening."

"We're not here to make you relive what happened to you." He almost cringed, seeing the lie in his words. "We just need your help." With a breath, he continued. "He's attacked another woman. He left her to die, Samantha, but she didn't. She fought like hell to stay alive, just as you did."

Another long silence, this time broken by the sound of a lock being grated open again. When the door opened, she still held the gun, but at her side this time.

"Why are you telling me this?" she whispered, her face wrought with emotion.

"Because you're the only one who can help us."

Wariness and fear battled in her gaze. "Help you do what, Agent Corwin?"

He drew in another breath. "Help us catch him."

She shouldn't have let them in. She shouldn't be making coffee for them, shouldn't allow them to sit in her living room as if they belonged there, as if what they had to say was of any interest to her.

Sam stood at the cedar work island in the middle of the spacious country kitchen, hands trembling as she reached for the handle of the coffee urn. As she poured the hot coffee into one of the mugs she'd grabbed from the cabinet, it spilled over the rim and splashed onto the counter. She watched the brown liquid soak into the wood.

God, when she'd looked out the window and seen those two men charging up her driveway…her heart had nearly stopped beating.

And then when they'd uttered her name—her real name—the fear had tripled. Nobody was supposed to know where she was, just the people sworn to protect her.

She shot a glance through the open doorway at the two men on her beige sofa, then stifled a sigh. FBI. That did make them her protectors. She guessed. But the desperation she'd seen in their eyes once she'd opened that door told her this visit wasn't about keeping her out of harm's way.

It was the exact opposite.

She wiped up the coffee stain as best as she could, then quickly filled the other mugs, set them on a tray and walked into the living room.

"Thank you," said the blond-haired man as she handed him a cup. Rick Scott, he'd said his name was. He looked pleasant enough, his smile genuine, but it was the other man who captured Sam's attention.

Tall, dark and handsome—a cliché, but one that suited him oh so well. Hair the color of rich chocolate, probably in need of a haircut, since it fell onto his forehead whenever he moved his head. But the scruffy look fit him, made his black trousers, white button-down shirt and sports coat seem less conservative—it gave him an edge. His eyes were a deep whiskey color, but when she looked closer, she could see the flecks of amber around his pupils.

Sinking into the armchair farthest from the sofa, she watched as Blake Corwin reached for his coffee. Even in his sports coat, she could tell that his arms were powerful, muscled. His wide chest and broad shoulders exuded the same power. Even though he was a complete stranger, his big strong body and intense brown eyes made her feel—for the moment—protected.

And...aroused?

No, impossible.

Leaning back in the chair, she would've liked to analyze her odd reaction further, that little flicker of heat that sparked in her belly at the sight of him, but Rick Scott spoke before she could do that.

"We apologize for showing up like this," he said, his voice gentle and soothing, giving Sam the sense that he had a lot of practice talking to victims.

Victim. The word loitered in her brain like a stray dog looking for scraps. Was that what she was? A victim? Swallowing back the acid creeping up her throat, she resisted the urge to shake her head. No, not a victim. A survivor.

"But we're running out of time," Blake Corwin finished.

She liked his voice. Not as gentle as his partner's, it had a husky, almost raspy quality to it. Sexy, most women would probably say.

Blake set down his mug on the small cedar coffee table and directed that intense gaze at her. "He grabbed a woman named Elaine Woodman from her office in downtown Chicago. It was one-thirty in the afternoon, and no one saw a thing."

Sam fingered the long white scar on the inside of her wrist, disturbed by what he'd said. "That's unusual, isn't it? For him, anyway."

He nodded. "The others were attacked in their homes, always at night. We're not sure why he just changed his MO like that."

"And she survived the attack?" She rubbed the scar, its texture jagged and bumpy under the pad of her thumb.

"Miraculously," Blake answered. His expression grew somber. "He left her in an abandoned warehouse, probably assuming she'd bleed to death. But he underestimated Elaine. Somehow she managed to crawl out and drag herself onto the street. A jogger found her and called 9-1-1."

"She lost so much blood that the doctors were surprised she managed to recover," Rick added.

Sam stopped toying with the scar, clasped her hands on her waist and bit her lower lip. Why were they telling her this? Didn't they care what it was doing to her? When she'd first seen them on her doorstep, she'd assumed they'd come to take yet another statement from her. That's why she'd been antagonistic, why her guard had shot up. Because the idea of telling her gruesome story even one more time was about as appealing as eating dirt. But no, they were here to tell her about another woman's horror, which was equally upsetting, if not more so.

Leaning forward, she fumbled for her coffee, gripped the mug between fingers that had suddenly grown icier than the air outside. A puff of steam rose from the cup and moistened the tip of her nose.

After taking a brief sip, she focused her gaze on the two men again. "I'm glad she's all right," she finally said, not quite sure why her voice sounded so cold.

"She's not all right," Blake corrected, his eyes meeting hers and holding. "Physically, yes, she's recovering, but—"

The loud ring of the telephone cut him off, but Sam made no move to reach for the cordless phone sitting on the table. Both agents watched her expectantly, waiting, but they sat motionless. It was only when the answering machine switched on that she acted.

"Lori, it's Virginia. I don't mean to frighten you, but I saw a strange car pulling into your driveway, and I just wanted to make sure—"

Sam clicked the "on" button and pressed the phone to her ear. "Hi, Virginia, sorry, I didn't make it to the phone in time."

The relief in her elderly neighbor's voice was unmistakable. "Is everything all right, Lori? I saw an unfamiliar car and I was scared it might be burglars."

Considering that the town of Wellstock boasted a crime rate of zero, Sam managed a chuckle. "No need to worry, Ginny. I'm fine. Some friends of mine just came to visit, that's all."

"Oh, good. You know I don't like knowing you're out there in that big house all by yourself."

"Don't worry, I'm all right. But thanks for calling."

Sam said goodbye and hung up, then turned to her visitors. "My neighbor," she explained.

Neither man commented on the fact that she'd been screening her calls. These days the phone didn't ring much, but when it did, she never picked up until she heard a familiar voice on the machine. Not until she was absolutely certain that whoever was on the other end couldn't hurt her. But no matter how recognizable the voice, she still experienced a tremor of fear each time she heard the name Lori Kendall.

God, she *wished* she could be Lori Kendall. Lori was a writer from Chicago who'd moved out to this farmhouse because she was tired of urban life. She was working on a new novel about the love affair between a Nazi soldier and a Jewish peasant in war-torn Germany, and she was so wrapped up in her work that she never went into town or struck up friendships with the Wellstock residents. But they all understood because writers, after all, were a strange breed.

Sam didn't know if the cover story made her feel like laughing or crying. The life the Bureau had given her was so different from the one she'd led before the attack, but it was a life she now wished she'd chosen for herself. Lori, the writer, would never have encountered a flesh-and-blood killer, only the ones she wrote about in her books.

But she wasn't really Lori, was she? No, she was Samantha Dawson, and the alias she'd received from the Witness Protection Program was just another reminder of the danger she still faced. Would probably always face, as long as the man who'd hurt her was on the loose.

Crossing her legs, Sam raked her fingers through her long hair and sighed. "Where were we? Right, his latest victim."

She sounded cold again, even a little indifferent, but she couldn't help it. She didn't want these men knowing that everything about this visit scared the crap out of her. She didn't want them to know that talking and hearing about another woman being attacked in the same way paralyzed her with fear. Better to let them think she didn't care, that she was over it, so far past it she didn't give a damn anymore.

"Elaine Woodman is in bad shape," Blake said, the determination in his eyes giving way to weariness. "She refuses to talk about what happened to her, and we know she's holding back details that could break this investigation. She's too scared, won't trust anyone to help her. It's almost as if she thinks that as long as she pretends it didn't happen, it will all go away."

Sam stared at the agent, amazed by his cavalier tone. A

slow and steady rush of anger coiled in the pit of her stomach and spiraled up her chest until all she could do was snap, "Of course she's scared. She's goddamn terrified!"

Slamming her cup on the table, she jumped out of her chair and took two steps toward Blake Corwin. "You actually blame her for that?" she demanded, her body simmering with rage. "For wanting to forget what happened? Well, she has every right to forget. She has every right not to want to talk to a bunch of egomaniacal shrinks and overeager cops who don't give a damn about her. You think she wants to spill her guts to a complete stranger and relive every sickening thing that man did to her? Of course she doesn't."

Sam snapped her mouth shut and strode toward the window on stiff legs, gluing her gaze to the barren front yard. She couldn't believe the nerve of these men, looking like a couple of wounded children over the "annoying" notion that a woman who'd nearly died refused to talk to them. Jerks. Insensitive jerks.

Anger continued to swirl inside her, but it was surprisingly welcome. For the first time in months she was experiencing something that wasn't fear or pain or self-pity. She wondered if it might have helped to be angry all those months ago, if maybe letting out her fury over what happened to her could've helped her heal faster.

As it was now, she didn't feel healed or cured or even convinced in the slightest that she could ever get over this.

But the anger helped. Just a little.

"That's why we came to see you."

Blake's voice remained steady, entirely unaffected by her incensed words. She turned around slowly and let their gazes connect again. Searched his magnetic eyes and found nothing more than that cool, calm and collected glint.

Never breaking eye contact, he clasped his hands on his lap and added, "We want you to see Elaine Woodman. We want you to break her silence."

Chapter 2

The guard she'd briefly let down snapped back up. With methodical steps, Sam walked back to the armchair and sank into it. "You want me to see her?" The words squeaked out slowly, laced with disbelief rushing through her veins.

Blake simply nodded.

"Why?" was all she asked.

"Because you know better than anyone what Elaine is going through," Blake said matter-of-factly. He leaned forward, causing the material of his jacket to stretch over his broad shoulders.

This time she couldn't deny the spark of attraction she felt at the sight of his powerful muscles constricting against his shirt. He was a sexy man. A very sexy man. Yet even admitting the obvious seemed inappropriate under these circumstances, after the bomb he'd just dropped in her lap.

She forced her gaze away from his chest, set her jaw and waited for him to continue.

"Elaine needs to feel safe when she finally decides to talk about her experience."

A low, bitter laugh slipped out before she could stop it. "Safe? You think she'll ever really feel safe?"

For the first time since he'd shown up at her door, Blake's features softened. The sympathy in his gaze reached out and touched her like the caress of a warm hand on her cheek. Ordinarily, she would have grown defensive, sickened by the sympathy, the pity. But strangely enough, the soft understanding in his dark eyes only eased her nerves.

"No," he said quietly. "I don't think she'll ever feel safe, not for a long time at least. But while this guy is still out on the streets, none of the women in Chicago will be safe, either."

"Why are you so sure Elaine Woodman can give you some information you don't already have?" She didn't mean to pose a challenge, yet somehow it came out that way.

"Because she's different," Blake replied without hesitation. "He took her in broad daylight and dumped her on the other side of the city, which means he had to have means of transporting her there. He didn't do that with any of the other victims."

"Elaine can provide us with details that might help us stop him once and for all," Rick added. "The kind of car he drives, any places he might have stopped at before dumping her."

"But she won't talk," Sam said grimly.

"Not to us." Blake paused, watching her. "But she might talk to you."

She took a breath, suddenly feeling torn. If this were just about her, about her own pain and suffering, she might've been able to say no, tell them to leave her alone and to hell with their investigation. But it wasn't just about her. There was another woman involved. Another survivor.

Her mind flashed back to the first day after the attack. She'd been lying in that hospital bed, staring at the dull white walls, unwilling to let anyone catch a glimpse of what she'd gone through. Even her brother, Beau, her only living relative, hadn't been able to penetrate the iron shield she'd erected around herself.

For days she'd lain motionless in bed, trying to forget, trying to trick herself into believing that such an unthinkably heinous act hadn't happened to her, not to *her*. And if it weren't for a kindhearted cop named Annette Hanson, she might have drowned in her own pain. Annette had helped her, drawn her out of the shell of self-preservation she'd hidden within, and though it was months before she'd been ready to live her life again, she knew she'd never be able to repay Annette for what she'd done.

Could she really let another woman drown the way she almost had?

Helping Elaine Woodman would no doubt bring back a rush of terrifying memories that Sam desperately wanted to forget, but would it be worth it, knowing she'd contributed to Elaine's healing process?

Drawing in a long breath, she eyed the men in front of her. "I…I'm going to need some time to think about it."

"There isn't any time." Blake knew his voice sounded harsh, but it needed to be said. The longer Elaine Woodman kept quiet, the greater the danger and the longer this killer had to find himself another victim.

He didn't blame Samantha for being uncertain. Hell, he'd read her file, seen photos of what that bastard had done to her. The woman had been hovering between life and death before the paramedics had shown up. How she'd managed to call the police, especially in her condition, still amazed him. All he knew was that Samantha Dawson possessed a strength that most people only wished they had.

His heart squeezed as he remembered another woman who'd exuded that same strength. Kate Manning, the woman whose death had caused him to dive headfirst into this case and push himself to the point of exhaustion simply to keep the memories at bay.

Not that it was helping. The memories continued to assault his mind anyway. It seemed as if everything and everyone reminded him of Kate, and, not for the first time, he wondered if maybe the Bureau shrink was right. Maybe there was no distraction great enough to make him forget.

He clenched his fists at the ominous notion. Lord, he couldn't do this now, couldn't think of Kate or that damn shrink. Not now. So he forcibly shoved the unwelcome thoughts from his head and tried to focus on the woman in front of him.

She seemed so cool, so controlled. He saw it in the way she sat, with her hands loosely draped over her lap. The way she spoke in that calm, even voice. The way she looked at him with those unwavering gray eyes. It seriously impressed him, but it didn't totally convince him, either. The little ragged breaths and the way her shoulders trembled almost imperceptibly at every sound told him that she was still terrified.

"If you're worried about your own safety," Rick said, "I can assure you we'll take every precaution to keep you protected."

With a chuckle, she muttered, "Right, because I'm supposed to be dead. Wonder how I overlooked that little tidbit?" She focused those haunting eyes on Blake. "How do you plan on taking me into the city without being recognized?"

If Rick was insulted by her intense focus on his partner, he didn't show it. Instead, he leaned back and let Blake field that question.

"We'll do whatever it takes," he said roughly, inwardly wondering why her impenetrable gaze made his palms grow damp. "We'll get you a disguise, bring you into the hospital after visiting hours, anything to protect your identity."

"My face will still be familiar—to most men, at least."

Her tone was dry, almost comical, and Blake fought the tiny grin tugging at the corners of his mouth. "Your face is probably not as recognizable as you think."

The comment, with its slightly lewd undertones, did not seem to faze her. Instead, she just nodded. "Quite true, Agent Corwin. But I'm not sure I'm willing to take that chance."

They'd reached an impasse. Blake knew that pushing her any further would only make her less likely to cooperate. Helping them had to be her choice. The ball was in her court now.

Blake exchanged a glance with Rick before rising from the sofa. "All right, we'll give you some time to think about this then," he said. "But don't take too long."

She offered an odd little smile. "Time is of the essence, right?"

"I'm afraid so."

He reached into his pocket and removed his card and a pen. He scribbled down both his and Rick's cell numbers, then handed it to her. She seemed to make an effort not to let their fingers brush as she accepted the card, and, for some reason, that bothered him a little.

"Just give us a call when you've made up your mind. But if we haven't heard from you by tomorrow afternoon, we'll need to get back to Chicago and explore other avenues."

The two men said their goodbyes and headed for the door. Samantha followed them, shotgun again in hand. After they'd stepped onto the porch, Blake heard all the various locks and safety mechanisms being clicked back into place.

As they descended the steps, Rick shot him a questioning look. "You think she'll help us?"

The snow crunching under his boots, Blake simply nodded. "Yes, I think she will."

"You really don't need to worry," Sam told her brother over the phone an hour after Blake and Rick had left the farmhouse.

She settled onto the couch and tucked her knees under her, then reached to flick on the lamp sitting on the end table. The late-afternoon sun was beginning to set and the absence of light streaming in from the windows made her muscles tense. Soon the sun would disappear altogether, leaving nothing but an inky black sky and menacing shadows.

She'd already turned on the main light. It bathed the room in a pale-yellow glow, but she didn't feel at ease unless every light in the house was on, too.

The darkness still bothered her, ever since that warm May night when she'd walked into her bedroom and seen the dark figure looming in the shadows. She slept with the light on now. Scratch that—she *lay in bed* with the light on. She didn't sleep. If she was lucky, she got five hours of rest a night, spread out in twenty-minute intervals because every time the REM cycle kicked in, she'd jerk herself awake. The nights were the hardest, always bringing with them a threat that she couldn't ignore.

"What do you mean, I don't have to worry?" Beau replied. "At the moment, that's exactly what I should be doing."

She smiled to herself, knowing without having to see him that there was a telltale crease in his forehead. Most times Beau's face was unreadable. Dark, stoic eyes, firm set of the mouth. But that little crease always gave him away. She'd seen it enough times growing up, and right now she heard it in his voice.

"Everything's fine," she assured him. "They were FBI agents, no danger to me."

"I disagree. The very fact that they want you to go into the city is dangerous."

"They said they'd protect me."

"Do you believe them?"

Sam remembered Blake Corwin's determined brown eyes. "Yes. I think they'll do everything in their power to keep me safe."

"And what if everything in their power isn't good enough?" Beau countered, his concern palpable over the airwaves. "What if someone recognizes you and calls the press? If this guy finds out that you didn't die that night…" He let his voice trail off ominously.

For the thousandth time in six months, Sam wished she'd never chosen such a high-profile career. Why hadn't she gone into accounting? Why on earth had she decided to model swimsuits of all things? She'd always done well in school, her grades good enough to get her into any college, but it had been the excitement of stardom that appealed to her the most. It helped that she had a body that was, as her friends always told her, designed to make men drool. She'd never minded flaunting it, strutting in front of a camera and making herself a public figure.

But she regretted it now. Although the police had assured her that it was unlikely the guy picked her just because of her celebrity status, she still got the feeling that she might have gone unnoticed, flitted under the bastard's radar, if she'd just chosen another field.

"It's a risk, I know." Her voice softened. "But I keep thinking about that woman, Beau."

Compassion filled his voice. "I know you want to help her, but at what cost, Sammy? Goddamn it, I can't let myself even think about losing you. I almost did once—I'd rather not go through that again."

She understood her brother's concerns, and knew where they came from. Even before their parents died in a car accident nearly a decade ago, Sam and Beau had only relied on each other. Growing up with workaholic parents who couldn't concern themselves with their children, she and her brother had formed a strong bond. As kids they'd banded together against their strict nanny, as teenagers they'd rebelled when their parents tried to force law school down their throats, and as adults they'd only grown closer. Beau was her constant pillar of support and the only person in her life who offered the unconditional love her mother and father hadn't been capable of.

The first couple of months after the attack had been tough for him. For her, too. The Bureau had encouraged her to cut off contact with Beau, worried that the man who'd tried to kill her might be watching her brother. They'd kept surveillance on Beau for as long as they could justify the cost, but after months without any sign of the Rose Killer, they'd finally called off the guards. It was still too dangerous for Beau to drive up to see her, but they were allowed to speak on the phone now. And each time they hung up, he always made sure to tell her he loved her, as if he were afraid that if he didn't he'd never get the chance again.

She knew he was scared for her, worried, uneasy about this situation. Hell, so was she. But Beau would never understand what Elaine Woodman was feeling at the moment.

Only she understood.

"I want to help her," she finally said, balancing the cordless on her shoulder so she could wrap her arms tightly around her knees. "I want to help catch this guy."

"Revenge, justice—is that it?"

"No, not entirely. I'm just...sick of living in fear." She exhaled shakily. "I can't do this anymore. I can't live in this isolated old house, miles away from civilization. I can't keep jumping at every noise and shadow. I can't put my life on hold anymore."

Beau made a frustrated sound. "Don't tell me you want to start modeling again."

Even if I did, I can't.

The silent reminder only made her eyes sting. No, she wouldn't cry, wouldn't give that bastard the satisfaction of crying one more tear. What he'd done to her had ensured that she'd never be able to model again, though only the hospital staff was aware of that. The nurses had seen the scar; of course, they'd been polite enough not to comment. But every time she stepped out of the shower she was reminded that her career was over.

Right now, however, that didn't matter.

"I'll never model again. But that doesn't mean I can't do something else. I've been thinking a lot lately about writing a novel." She laughed humorlessly. "I'm supposed to be a writer now—might as well live the lie."

"Then write a book. You don't need to go back to Chicago to do it. Just lie low until this psychopath is caught."

"But what if I can help catch him?"

Beau grew silent. She could picture the crease in his forehead growing deeper, more defined. "You've already made up your mind, haven't you?"

"Yeah, I guess I have."

* * *

The pressure in Blake's temples eased the second he hung up the phone. A grim smile crossed his mouth as his partner's words echoed in his head. *She says she'll do it.*

He'd known she would, had sensed that Samantha Dawson wasn't the type to sit idly by and twiddle her thumbs while the maniac who'd nearly killed her roamed the streets. He hadn't, however, expected her to make up her mind so soon.

Hadn't expected her to call Rick, either.

Shrugging out of his shirt, he headed for the motel's tiny bathroom, which was no bigger than a closet and made him feel slightly claustrophobic. As he tugged at the zipper of his pants, he couldn't help but frown. It shouldn't bother him that Samantha had called to tell Rick what she'd decided to do, and not him. Both his and Rick's numbers had been printed on that business card—so what if she hadn't dialed his?

Still frowning, he stepped into the minuscule shower and turned on the faucet. He wondered, as the warm water splashed down his body, if it was inappropriate to be turned on by the woman.

Probably.

No, absolutely.

She was a victim, after all. Not to mention a witness in his case, which made his desire for her not only inappropriate but unethical.

You've been celibate for too long.

Blake reached for the small complimentary shampoo bottle, squeezed a glob into his hands, then lathered his hair. Celibacy. It wasn't a state he liked, but since this damn case began sex was the last thing on his mind.

He'd learned the hard way what happened when he indulged in sex and relationships during a case. When he'd first joined the Bureau it had been easy separating his job from his personal life; back then his cases had hardly been life-threatening.

But when he'd transferred to the "Serial Squad," as Rick jokingly referred to their unit, Blake's ability to compartmentalize had been blown to bits. Bigger cases meant higher stakes. Higher stakes meant no distractions. And he quickly learned that his personal life was a distraction he couldn't afford.

If she were alive, Kate Manning could probably vouch for that.

Hard as he tried to stop it, the thought of Kate slid into his head, making him sag against the tiled wall. He'd been thinking about her a lot lately. Too much. Probably because this case reminded him of the case he'd been working when Katie died. The Rose Killer was as sadistic as the man Blake had killed two years ago, the man Kate had been profiling for him.

He dunked his head under the stream of hot water and tried to clear his mind of the serious redhead who'd gotten under his skin and grabbed hold of his heart. The serious redhead who was dead because of him.

This time he paid attention to the authoritative voice in his head. Yes, he had to focus. He had a case to solve. A witness to protect.

And feeling any sort of attraction to that witness was out of the question.

"God help me," he muttered, his voice sounding oddly muted in the enclosed space.

Shutting off the water, he stepped out of the stall and wrapped a towel around his waist. Then he wiped away the steam on the mirror and examined his foggy reflection, wondering if he appeared as tired to others as he did to himself. Because, hell, he *was* tired. Tired and bone-weary and so close to the breaking point he could practically feel the ground under him beginning to give in. If they didn't get a lead in this case—and soon—he knew he'd burn out. He just hoped he could hold on a little while longer.

"Whoa! Keep that towel on, pal," Rick cried as Blake walked out of the bathroom.

Quickly tightening the terry cloth over his lower body, Blake stared at the blond man sitting on his bed as if he owned it. "How the hell did you get in here?" he demanded.

Rick shrugged. "You left the door unlocked."

"And the concept of privacy never entered your tiny pea of a brain before you waltzed in here?"

"Nope." Rick grinned. "My pea brain and I wanted to talk to you about Samantha Dawson."

Blake sighed. "Let me put on some clothes first."

After he'd changed into a pair of gray sweatpants and a faded black T-shirt, he stepped back into the small room.

Rick was still lounging on the bed, so Blake headed for the stained table in the corner and sat in one of the plastic chairs. The room was far too cramped for his liking, but what else could he expect from the only motel in Wellstock?

"So I figured we'd pass her off as Elaine Woodman's sister," Rick started, getting right to the point. He crossed one leg over the other, looking as uncomfortable on the hard mattress as Blake knew he'd feel sleeping on it. "As much as I like the doctor treating Elaine, I don't want him knowing who Samantha is."

"He's been really good about keeping Elaine's presence a secret," Blake said, then paused. "Mel's still posing as a nurse there, right?"

"Knight plans to keep her there until Elaine is ready to be discharged. From what Mel says, Elaine is safe."

He didn't miss the way Rick briefly averted his eyes at the

mention of Melanie Barnes. A subtle hint, but it wasn't the first time Blake suspected that Rick and their fellow agent might be romantically involved. He just hoped his partner knew what he was doing. Rick's divorce wasn't even final yet, and from what Blake knew about Patty Scott, he had a feeling the woman wouldn't hesitate to squeeze more cash out of her ex if she knew he was seeing another woman.

"Well, at least the media camped outside have no idea Elaine is alive."

"Then why don't they get the hell out of there?" Rick grumbled.

"We both know why. They're hoping to find someone in the hospital willing to give them details. Maybe even autopsy photos."

Rick shook his head in disgust. "That's sick, man."

"Don't tell me." Blake rubbed his eyes. "If even one picture of Samantha is taken, however unintentionally… All we need is one nosy reporter taking a good look and thinking, 'Hey, she looks familiar.'"

"I know." Rick's expression grew serious. "We'll have to take her in from the back, maybe through a service elevator. Give her some dark glasses, a wig, alter her appearance with makeup." He shrugged. "Elaine's doctor won't object to sneaking her in. We'll also try to bring her after visiting hours, when fewer reporters will be around, and we'll make sure Mel is on duty, just in case."

Blake's headache reappeared as swiftly as it had disappeared. Temples pounding like a tribal drum, he went over the plan in his head. Chances were, nobody in the hospital would even be aware of Samantha's presence, and if they were, her cover as the sister of a patient wouldn't raise any suspicions. Yet it still worried him, plucking Samantha from her safe, isolated farmhouse and shoving her right back into the path of a killer.

"She'll be okay." As usual, Rick seemed to read his mind.

"One visit," Blake muttered. "That's all we can allow. One visit to try to get Elaine to open up. After that, Samantha returns to this invisible town and goes back to being Lori Kendall until this guy is caught."

Rick nodded in agreement. "That's the plan."

They both grew quiet, somber, and Blake used the silence to go over all the possible risks they might face in bringing Samantha into Chicago. He figured his partner was doing the same, so he was surprised when Rick, in a low voice, uttered, "She's gorgeous, isn't she?"

Well, at least he wasn't the only one who'd noticed.

"Yeah." His voice came out rough.

"I subscribed to *Sports Illustrated* just to see her spreads in the swimsuit edition," Rick admitted, looking sheepish. "That is, until Patty canceled my subscription. But those photos…man. Always classy, sensual as hell, but classy."

It struck Blake as odd, even wrong, that they were discussing her in this way. She may have been a sexy model in her past life, but in *this* life she was a victim and a witness. Hardly deserving of their scrutiny, even if it was appreciative.

"You think she'll go back to modeling when this is all over?" Rick asked.

The question brought a cheerless smile to his lips. "I doubt it."

"Because of the scars? There are surgeries available these days that can remove them."

"After what that bastard did to her, I don't think she'll ever want to put herself on display again."

A lump of sadness lodged in the back of his throat, not so

much for Samantha Dawson as for all the other victims. The Rose Killer didn't try to hide his handiwork—hell, he seemed damn proud of what he did. When Blake saw the first victim's body, he'd been sickeningly amazed by the sheer intricacy of the carvings. Though they were still unsure of what it all meant, for some inexplicable reason, the bastard had a fascination with roses.

Why else would he carve them into his victims' skin?

At least Samantha had been spared the full effect of the killer's madness. Blake had been surprised when he'd studied her photos and seen only one rose. The profilers at Quantico suspected that the lack of mutilation had something to do with the fact that Samantha's body was "well known." Maybe the guy wanted to keep her as untainted as possible; maybe he thought a body like hers deserved to remain uncluttered. Who the hell knew? Blake didn't need to be a profiler to figure out that this killer was a monster. Analyzing his motives didn't tell them anything they didn't already know.

Yet the guy was human. He had to be. Because humans made mistakes, and this guy had already made two big ones. He'd inadvertently left Samantha Dawson and Elaine Woodman alive, and in the end, that's what would finally put him behind bars.

Chapter 3

"Where's your partner?" Sam asked the next afternoon. She peered past Blake's impressively broad shoulders in search of Rick Scott. All she saw was a heap of fresh powdery snow and her barren yard. A black SUV idled in front of her garage, and when she glanced through the tinted windows, she realized that Blake had come here alone.

"We came up in separate cars in case one of us needed to leave," he answered. "Rick drove back to Chicago last night to get a few things in order before we bring you to the hospital."

He shoved his hands into the pockets of his faded blue jeans, and her gaze instantly took in how snugly the denim fit against his powerful legs. He looked good in jeans. And the thick cable-knit sweater that stretched over his lean chest looked darn good, too.

She was a little startled to notice how tall he was. He'd been sitting down during most of yesterday's visit, and now, standing right next to him, she was able to appreciate the sheer size of him. He was at least six-three, but there was nothing bulky about him, just a broad chest that tapered into a lean waist, and a whole slew of sculpted muscles. God, this man had the whole package, didn't he? Classically handsome features, drool-worthy body.

"Are you ready to go?"

Their eyes locked, and his slightly wry expression told her that he'd caught her studying him. An unexplained rush of heat scorched her cheeks, which only reddened further when she remembered the dream she'd had last night.

Blake. Kissing her. Just a soft, slow kiss, a far cry from those sweeping cinematic kisses that left the audience in breathless awe, but it had enough of an effect on her that she hadn't been able to get the dream out of her mind all morning.

She hadn't felt anything close to desire for a man since the attack, and it shocked her that her body was capable of producing such a reaction. Hell, it had surprised her so much she'd actually jarred herself awake from the disturbing dream, heart pounding and brain demanding to know how she could envision such a thing.

Six months ago, the thought of kissing a man wouldn't have scared her. Though she was far from promiscuous, she'd had her share of lovers, and she'd certainly enjoyed making love. Until her entire life had shattered before her eyes. Now, the thought of being with a man came with fear that gnawed at her like a raccoon in a trash can. Aside from her brother, any man who came into her presence brought on terrifying suspicion, bone-deep worry that he might hurt her.

So why wasn't she scared of *this* man?

"Samantha?"

"What? Oh, sure, I'm ready. Let me just lock up."

She could feel Blake's intense gaze on her as she stuck her key in a lock and latched the front door. She slung the strap of her overnight bag over her shoulder before following Blake down the porch steps toward his SUV.

She'd already called Virginia and informed her that she'd be out of town for a couple of days. Her excuse had been that she was going to Chicago to do some research for her novel, and her neighbor had wished her luck and demanded a copy of the book when it was released. Although she hadn't gone out of her way to be friendly with anyone in town, Sam knew the older woman cared about her, and it reassured her knowing that someone would keep an eye out for any strangers who might approach the house in her absence.

"Here, let me put this in the back," Blake said, reaching for her bag.

Their fingers brushed as he took it, and for one brief second, Sam faltered. It wasn't as if she'd expected a spark of electricity or anything, but the feel of his warm hand grazing hers was just as alarming.

Trying not to focus on anything other than the reason she was going with him, she sank into the passenger seat of the car and settled into the cushy leather interior. Blake closed the trunk and rounded the vehicle. From the corner of her eye, she saw him slide into the seat next to her.

"How's your butt?"

Indignation colored her cheeks. "Excuse me?"

For the first time since they'd met, he shot her a grin. "I mean, is it cold or anything? This car has top-of-the-line seat warmers. I could turn yours on if you'd like."

"Oh. No, that's okay," she stammered, still feeling winded by the unexpected smile tugging on the corners of his mouth. Lord, this man looked gorgeous when he smiled.

"Suit yourself." He shrugged and turned on the ignition, then pressed a button under the dashboard and gave a contented sigh. "God bless seat warmers."

Oh to be the seat under that man's ass.

The sly little thought popped into her head before she could stop it. It was exactly the type of thing she would've thought once upon a time, when she'd had a successful modeling career and a parade of men at her door. Her best friend, Susan, had always teased her about the mischievous little comments she'd used to make.

God, she missed the days when she'd been…carefree. Happy. She missed Susan, too, but she knew that temporarily severing ties with the people in her life was for the best.

She leaned against the soft headrest behind her, shooting Blake a sideways glance as he backed out of the driveway and turned the SUV around. They didn't speak as he drove down the icy road. She listened to the sound of snow crunching underneath the tires and the soft strains of country music floating out of the stereo speakers.

Her pulse quickened the moment they turned onto the main street leading toward the highway. She inhaled slowly, willing her pulse to slow. She didn't want Blake to know that the thought of returning to civilization scared the crap out of her.

"It'll be okay, Samantha."

His quiet voice and words of reassurance made surprise jolt through her. Had he read her mind, or was her fear written on her face? She hadn't thought it was, but since the idea of her features giving her away wasn't as unsettling as the idea of Blake finding a way into her head, she preferred to consider herself transparent.

"Sam," she finally said, not responding to his astute remark. "You can call me Sam."

"All right. It'll be okay, Sam," he repeated.

"I know." She blew out a shaky breath. "Of course it'll be okay."

He shot her a quick glance, the expression in his deep brown eyes telling her that he didn't quite believe her. "By this time tomorrow, you'll be back in your farmhouse, doing—what is it you do all the way out there? Puzzles, crosswords? Do you like to read?"

He was trying to distract her and they both knew it. But she welcomed the distraction nevertheless. "I read a lot, actually," she admitted, playing with the sleeve of her warm wool sweater.

"What do you read?" His voice remained relaxed, even as he turned onto the on ramp of the highway and easily merged with traffic.

Her gaze darted to the window, fixing on the cars and trucks and vans whizzing by. Her pulse accelerated, just a little, at the sounds of tires squealing and horns blaring, at the sight of faceless, nameless people driving alongside them. Overhead, the late-afternoon sun disappeared behind a patch of thick gray clouds the moment they picked up speed. An omen of things to come?

Pushing aside the disturbing notion, she focused on Blake's question. "I like mysteries. Some romance."

"Bodice-rippers, huh?"

"Why do men always call them that?"

He chuckled. "Because the covers always depict a half-naked Fabio ripping the bodice off a fair maiden."

"Well, what do you like to read? Or are you too busy for that?"

"You hit the nail on the head with that one. With my caseload, I'm lucky if I get past the first page of a novel. I used to read a lot of thrillers though."

"Is that why you do this job, for the thrills?"

The question slipped out before she could stop it, but she regretted it the second his voice turned harsh. "There's nothing thrilling about chasing monsters."

She drew in a breath. "I…you're right. I shouldn't have said that. I'm sorry."

She heard him take a breath of his own. "No, I'm the one who should be sorry. I shouldn't have snapped at you."

Out of newfound habit, her fingers slid down to her wrist and rubbed that irritating scar. For a long while they drove in silence before she said, "You've been after him a long time, haven't you?"

He didn't need to ask her who *he* was. "Almost eight months now."

Since she knew the murders had been going on for at least two months longer, she wrinkled her forehead. "Not from the beginning?"

Blake kept his eyes on the road. "The Chicago PD didn't call us in until the third victim was discovered. Once they realized they had a serial killer on their hands, they needed all the help they could get."

The third victim. It bothered her to hear him say that. First victim. Second. Third. As if they were nothing more than numbers. Not women who had once breathed, lived. Just numbers.

Was she a number? The fourth victim? Was that how Blake and his fellow agents referred to her?

"What was her name, the third victim?" she asked softly.

"Diana Barrett."

A tiny pang of guilt tugged at her insides when she realized that it was the first time she'd heard that name. She'd been so caught up in her own pain, her own ordeal, that she'd never really thought to ask about the others. Diana Barrett. Elaine Woodman. Hearing the names, knowing the identities of the other women, made her feel…less alone.

Another blare of a car horn caught her attention. This time the sound didn't make her flinch. This time the vehicles driving alongside them didn't evoke fear, but determination.

A sense of purpose surged through her, bringing with it a flicker of familiarity. She'd once been a woman who wasn't afraid to charge forward, take action and grab what she wanted out of life. A woman who hadn't let fear or doubt slow her down, or pulled the covers over her head when things got a little too rough.

She'd thought that woman had abandoned her the night she'd almost died, but she'd been wrong.

After the attack, she'd fled, hid from the world, clung to her fear, but now she found herself clutching the other side of the survival-instinct coin. Fight or flight. Last time she'd chosen the latter.

This time she was going to fight.

And every mile that brought them closer to the city she'd deserted strengthened her conviction that she was doing the right thing.

Blake instantly noticed the change in his passenger, the way her gray eyes had gone from dull to vibrant, the way she'd straightened her back and lifted her chin as if she were walking into battle. Something inside her had shifted, and he wondered if he'd played a part in it. He'd thought that talking about Diana Barrett would cause Sam to crawl back inside herself, but it seemed to have had just the opposite effect. She suddenly looked driven, confident and…sexy.

Don't even go there, man.

Trying not to admire her delicate profile, he focused on driving, the hour-long journey finally coming to an end as he steered the SUV onto a residential street.

Sam's demeanor quickly reverted back to the one he'd grown used to. Suspicious and uneasy.

"Where are we?"

"My house," he replied as he parked in the snow-covered driveway and shut off the engine.

She studied the modest two-story home intently. Her gaze flicked from the dark-red bricks to the white front door to the towering oak trees shielding the house from the road. After she'd finished her scrutiny, she turned to face him, still wary and now a little distrustful.

"Why are we here?"

He unbuckled his seat belt and reached for the door handle. "We can't take you to a hotel, Sam." He opened the door and got out, adding, "You're staying here with me."

He moved around the vehicle to open her door, but she unsnapped her seat belt and bounded out before he could reach for the handle. "I...why am I staying here?"

He didn't like the panic he saw in those smoky-gray eyes. Was she afraid of him?

Hell, he realized, of course she was. She was probably afraid of any male who came within a five-mile radius of her. And he didn't really blame her.

Keeping his tone gentle, he held her worried gaze. "We can't risk having anyone figure out who you are—you know that. Sending you to a farmhouse miles away from civilization is one thing, but if you waltz into a hotel and check in, even with an alias, you'd be taking a chance that someone might recognize you."

She swallowed. "I know."

"This is the only way to keep you safe." *As safe as you can be.*

"I know," she repeated.

Without any more objections, she hugged her chest with her arms and waited as he grabbed her bag from the trunk. Then she quietly followed him up the snowy path leading to the house.

He watched her from the corner of his eye, noting the protective way she held her arms, and his heart squeezed a little. Damn, he didn't know what it was about this woman, but she brought out a nurturing side in him that he didn't know he possessed. Every time he looked into those haunted eyes, he just wanted to pull her into his arms. He wanted to tell her that every goddamn thing was going to be all right, that the man who'd hurt her would be caught and punished, and that nothing—*nothing*—would ever hurt her again.

And he really wanted to kiss her.

A soundless groan lodged in the back of his throat. Great. As if he weren't stressed out enough. Now he had to deal with ridiculous urges more suited to a fifteen-year-old than a grown man who had a job to do.

He shouldn't be thinking about kissing this woman. Nobody could deny how stunning she was, but as a federal agent he should know better than to be captivated by a witness.

"Wow…I didn't expect…this," she marveled when they stepped into the front hall. She glanced at the wood-paneled walls, then down at the rich, red carpet beneath their feet. "It's so cozy in here."

Before he could answer, she shook off her black leather boots and brushed past him, looking, for the first time all day, interested in her surroundings. He suppressed a grin as he unlaced his own boots, then set the security alarm on the wall. When he entered the living room to see Sam examining the large stone fireplace in front of the brown leather couch, he had to smile.

"What were you expecting?" he asked curiously.

She whirled around, a tentative smile reaching her lips. "A bachelor pad," she admitted. "Bare necessities, couch, TV and table to put the beers on. But this place is amazing. Did you decorate it yourself?"

He chuckled, watching her stare at an oil painting—a landscape—hanging nearby. "I wish I could take credit, but my mother is the interior decorator in the family, not me. She came by and worked her magic. You should see my family home."

"So you live here in Chicago? Don't you work out of Quantico?" she asked.

He nodded. "I am in Virginia a lot, but I try to come back here whenever I can. That's why I bought this house, more of an incentive to come home."

"I've always loved this city," she confessed, sounding wistful. She moved over to the tall bookshelf in the corner and absently ran her fingers over the spines of the novels stacked there.

"I'd assume in your line of work, you'd be traveling to New York and L.A. quite a lot," he said. "What made you choose Chicago as your home base?"

He found himself oddly curious about this woman. What he knew about her came from her file, an array of facts compiled on paper. Sure, he was aware that she and her older brother had been orphaned when she was sixteen. Knew she'd gotten her first break when a talent agent discovered her in a shopping mall. Knew she looked damn good in swimsuits, and that her middle name was Corrine. Yet knowing and understanding were two different things.

For some inexplicable reason, he wondered about the woman behind the profile. How had she felt growing up with only her brother? Why had she chosen to become a model? Why hadn't there been a man in her life to help her heal after the attack?

That those questions should even be important to him was more troubling than he'd have liked to admit.

"I grew up here." She shrugged and met his eyes. "All the places I've traveled never seemed to compare. This is home. At least, it used to be."

He cleared his throat, knowing that he couldn't offer assurance that she'd be able to leave her farmhouse anytime soon. "Why don't you go upstairs and get settled?" he suggested. "You can take the guest room at the end of the hall."

She nodded. "All right. When are we going to the hospital?"

He glanced at his watch. Quarter to five. "Probably around nine," he answered. "Visiting hours end at eight but we want to make sure the press isn't lingering around when we get there. If it were up to me, we'd go much later, but Elaine's doctor says she needs to rest. No late-night visits."

"Have you met her before?" Sam's voice was soft.

"Yes."

Her knowing gaze told him she'd caught the hitch in his voice. "She's not in very good shape, is she?"

Blake swallowed. "No. She's not."

"Your name is Lois Lawford," Rick Scott said. He turned the key in the ignition and backed the unmarked sedan out of Blake's driveway. "You're Elaine's sister."

Sam managed a nod, her heartbeat accelerating and palms growing damp as she stared at Blake's house in the rearview mirror, slowly disappearing from sight. She felt like a kid on her first day of school, nervous, panicked over leaving behind the familiar and delving into the unknown. Only what lay in store for her wasn't a strange classroom and a bunch of kids she'd never met—she was about to meet a woman who'd suffered as much as she had. And the thought of looking into another survivor's eyes and seeing everything she herself had felt mere months ago was unbelievably nerve-wracking.

At least nobody would recognize her in this getup. The frumpy sweater and baggy jeans Rick had asked her to change into were uncomfortable, the short blond wig on her head was making her scalp itch and the thick black eyeglasses pinched her nose. A young female cop from the Chicago PD had stopped by Blake's house to apply Sam's makeup, and the woman had done a good job. Sam's complexion was now darker, hinting at Mediterranean descent. The shadows under her eyes gave her face a sunken look, and there was even a small mole over her top lip now. She'd barely recognized herself when she'd glanced in the mirror. The whole disguise made her feel homely and out of sorts.

Her nerves began to skitter as Rick drove in the direction of Chicago General. The last time she'd been there was as a patient, not a visitor, and those memories were far too fresh, far too raw, to forget. For a second she was tempted to order Rick to turn the car around and drive her back to Blake's where she'd felt safe, but she quickly tamped down the irrational urge.

It wasn't that she didn't want to help with the investigation. She would do anything to put the man who'd attacked her behind bars. But wanting to help and experiencing her own trauma again were two different things. Sure, she could browse through mug shots, hope to miraculously identify a man whose face she'd never even seen. But staring into the tortured eyes of another victim and hearing the tormenting tale that would no doubt mirror her own?

God, she didn't know if she could do it.

Hoping that talking about the investigation would ease her anxiety, she glanced at Rick. "Is Lois Elaine's older or younger sister?"

"Older. You're a journalist from DC, but weren't able to get away until now. You and Elaine were never really close." Rick smiled faintly. "I guess that sort of makes you insensitive, for not coming to see your sister sooner."

"As long as nobody finds out who I am, I'm fine with being seen as insensitive." She hesitated, briefly staring at the dark road ahead before turning back to Rick. "Why didn't Blake come with us?"

"He went on ahead. He's arranging for a couple of cops from the Chicago PD task force to keep an eye on the hospital entrance while you're inside. Just to make sure any reporters are kept in line."

"Oh."

Her hands trembled. She didn't know why Blake's absence bothered her, but it did. She'd come to trust Blake Corwin—at least as much as she could trust anyone. Something about his tall, powerful body made her feel protected, feel as if he would step in front of a bullet if it meant saving her life. Which was a little ironic, considering that, one, she barely knew the man, and, two, he'd put her in danger just by bringing her back here. By bringing her back from the dead.

"Wait, reporters?" she said suddenly, focusing on Rick's last remark. "Why would reporters be there? Elaine was declared dead."

Rick shrugged. "Hoping to get an interview with her doctor maybe, or find a nurse willing to talk about what happened. Elaine is in the ICU, pretty much the only area those vultures can't get into, so I don't think they suspect that she might be alive. I think they just want any scrap of information they can get about this case. A serial killer in Chicago?" His mouth twisted drily. "That's big news."

The hospital came into view, its lights illuminating the dark neighborhood. An ambulance whizzed past their car, sirens blaring as it sped toward the emergency entrance of the massive gray building.

Rick drove right past the main lot and toward a narrow alley in the back. The cargo area, she realized.

"He's not always so intense, by the way," Rick said suddenly.

She swallowed. "What?"

"Blake." He grinned. "He's not as intimidating as he'd like everyone to believe."

A half-mocking smile reached her lips. "Really? I would never have guessed."

Rick parked the car. "He's usually a lot more relaxed. Smiles more often, too. This case is really getting to him."

Boy, didn't she know it.

Rick unbuckled his seat belt and searched her face, his pale-blue eyes tinged with encouragement. "Are you ready?"

She took a breath. "Ready as I'll ever be."

Chapter 4

Getting to Elaine Woodman's room was surprisingly easy and went without a hitch. The orderly who'd met them hadn't seemed the least bit suspicious by her backdoor arrival. As it turned out, a few reporters were still hanging around the lobby, but on an unrelated case. Apparently, a popular movie star's wife had been admitted earlier in the evening, experiencing complications from a much-publicized pregnancy. Whether the orderly who let them in thought Sam was connected to that particular story, she didn't know. She didn't care, either, as long as she entered and left this hospital undetected.

She and Rick rode a service elevator up to the brightly lit ICU, where they were met by Henry Darwitz, Elaine's doctor. Sam introduced herself as Elaine's sister, and with a brisk nod, the doctor left her and Rick in front of Elaine's private room.

"Kira Lawford," she muttered, reading the chart hanging

by the door. She turned to the agent beside her. "Huh. Her alias is almost like mine, but with the initials flipped."

Rick shrugged. "I don't pick the names."

The sound of footsteps echoed in the deserted corridor and Sam instinctively glanced up. A petite blonde in a nurse's uniform walked past them, heading toward the nurses' station nearby. Sam's nerves eased as she saw the woman rummage around on the desk, her gaze never once drifting in their direction.

Turning around, Sam stared at the closed blinds over the window of Elaine's room, wishing she could peer through them to get a look at the woman inside. She wanted to be prepared when she walked in, wanted to see Elaine's face before she stirred up painful wounds.

"Do you think she'll talk to me?" she asked quietly.

Rick looked grim. "Let's hope so."

Taking a steadying breath, she reached for the door and slowly pushed it open.

Darkness engulfed her, and it took a moment for her eyes to adjust. Her gaze was drawn to the bed in the center of the room. Elaine Woodman lay there, a thin sheet pulled all the way up to her chin, her eyes closed. The way Elaine's honey-brown hair fanned across the stark white pillow made her look like a sleeping angel. Like nothing more than a pretty young woman dozing in her bed.

A voice suddenly ripped through the darkness. "Who are you?"

Sam took a step closer and found a pair of sharp green eyes zeroing in on her. Wary. Fearful. The slice of moonlight filtering in through the filmy curtains made those eyes appear larger, brighter, a vivid emerald tint that gave them a catlike quality.

"Did I wake you?" Sam asked, stepping toward the bed.

Elaine reached out and grasped the top of the sheet tighter, pulling it higher, and that's when Sam noticed the bandages on her slender wrists. Almost unconsciously, she glanced down at her own wrists, making out the jagged white scars even in the darkness.

"Who are you?" Elaine repeated, sliding up into a sitting position. "What do you want?"

The woman looked suspicious and terrified and reminded Sam so much of herself that she almost turned away. She'd been mistrustful of anyone who'd come into her hospital room, too, wondering if they wanted yet another statement, wishing they would let her lick her wounds in peace.

Knowing she was walking on eggshells, she simply stood next to the bed and offered a gentle smile. "My name is Samantha Dawson. You can call me Sam, though."

A flicker of recognition. "Do I know you?" Elaine sounded uncertain.

"No, we've never met. But if my name sounds familiar to you, it might be because you've heard it before. It probably came up when the detectives spoke to you."

Elaine went still, then broke the short silence with a sharp intake of breath. "You're…dead." Her pale face grew even paler. "Oh, Jesus, are you a ghost?"

Sam had to chuckle at that. With a smile, she sank onto the small metal chair next to the bed. "No, I can assure you that I'm not a ghost. See?" She reached out and lightly touched Elaine's upper arm, not surprised when the young woman recoiled. Pulling her hand back, she fought to keep the smile on her lips. "Flesh and blood, just like you."

"He attacked you, too," Elaine said bleakly. She wrapped her arms around her chest. "But you survived? Like me?"

"Yes. The police sent me into hiding after I left the hospital."

"So why are you here? Aren't you scared that…"

Elaine didn't finish her sentence, but Sam knew what she'd been going to say. *Aren't you scared that he'll come after you again?*

Her heart squeezed. Elaine's voice sounded so forlorn, so tortured. The voice of a woman who'd been hurt badly, whose youthful vitality had been sucked out of her. Sam knew the girl was twenty-three, but her tiny body, barely taking up any space on that narrow bed, made her appear younger, more vulnerable. The last thing Sam wanted to do was hurt this girl any more than she'd already been hurt.

Yet she didn't have a choice.

"Rick Scott and his partner asked me to come see you. You met them, right?"

Elaine nodded.

"Well, they thought I might be able to help you."

The girl's mouth twisted in self-loathing. "Nobody can help me."

Sam swallowed hard and raked her fingers through her hair, finding its texture different and remembering that she was wearing a wig.

"That's what I thought," she finally responded, "when I was lying here, in this same hospital, with those same bandages on my wrists. I thought my life was over. I didn't want to talk to anyone about what happened."

When Elaine remained quiet, she went on. "It's a terrible feeling, isn't it? Helplessness. Hopelessness."

Those big green circles penetrated her face. "You forgot fear."

"Trust me, I didn't forget."

"You're still scared?" The sheet covering Elaine's chest drooped as she leaned forward slightly, revealing another bandage, a bigger one, on her neck.

Sam knew exactly what lay beneath that gauze, but she forced herself to stay focused. "Yes, I'm still scared. The FBI has been keeping me hidden, but—" she took a breath "—I don't feel safe."

"Me, either," Elaine murmured. Her eyes grew glassy, and Sam knew she was on the verge of tears. "I'm leaving the hospital soon. Or at least, Kira Lawford is. I don't know where they're taking me."

"They're trying to protect you."

"By showing up here every day and trying to force me to talk to them?" Sarcasm laced her tone. "It doesn't feel like protection. More like pressure."

"I know."

"Did you enjoy it? Sitting there and spilling your guts, while some unfeeling cop took notes?"

"No, I didn't." She leaned forward and touched Elaine's hand. This time, the girl didn't pull away. "I hated it. I hated all of them. Except Annette Hanson. She was a cop, the only cop who was patient with me, who didn't force me to talk, didn't force me to do anything. She relocated to Indiana a few months ago, which is a shame. You would've liked her. It was Annette I finally confided in."

Elaine watched her knowingly. "And now I'm supposed to confide in you?"

"If you want." Sam squeezed her hand reassuringly. "You don't have to. If you want, we can talk about something else, just visit a little."

"You won't push me?"

"Of course not."

At that instant Sam knew without a doubt that Blake was not going to like this. Funny how she wasn't worried about Rick Scott's reaction, just Blake's.

Blake would've wanted her to push Elaine. Not because he was one of those "unfeeling" cops Elaine had described, but because Sam knew he'd wanted this to be a onetime deal. The plan had called for her to see Elaine tonight, try to get her to open up, and go back to Wellstock. Whether she succeeded or failed in getting through to Elaine didn't matter. She couldn't risk being recognized, and that meant one visit and one visit only.

But Sam wouldn't—she *couldn't*—leave it at that. The young girl sitting in front of her deserved better than that.

"I can come back to visit you as many times as you'd like," she said softly, trying not to think of Blake as she spoke. "I'm not here just because the police suggested I come, but because I think talking to me might help you. I understand what you're going through. I went through it. And I just want to help, that's all. No pressure."

Worry creased the girl's features. "Won't that be dangerous? For you, I mean? He—" Her voice cracked. "He thinks you're dead. He thinks *we're* dead."

"Are you worried that he'll come after you?"

A single tear slipped from one of those emerald eyes and slid down Elaine's pale cheek. "I haven't slept since it happened. I never stop thinking that he might come back to finish the job."

Sam's throat tightened as she saw Elaine's gaze drop to her wrists, and before she could analyze her motives, she shoved out her hands, displaying her own scars.

"He won't finish the job," she said firmly. "See these? He did the same thing to me, and look, they're healing, fading. Yours will, too. I promise you, that bastard will never hurt you again. *Never.*"

It was nearly midnight when Blake returned home. He'd driven back in his SUV, following Rick's dark sedan and wondering if Sam had managed to get any details from Elaine Woodman.

Not only had spending the evening watching the hospital entrance been uneventful, but it had been nerve-wracking as well. The paparazzi, merciless as usual, had snapped shots of anyone and everyone going in and out, hoping to land a scoop in the celebrity pregnancy story. Normally, Blake despised the media, but tonight all he'd cared about was making sure Sam's visit went unnoticed. Since Rick had called and informed him that everything had gone as planned, Blake wasn't worried any longer.

He was desperate as hell, though, to know what had transpired between Sam and Elaine. He prayed to God that she'd gotten through to her. Rick hadn't said a word about the visit, so Blake, during the entire drive home, was left to wonder.

He pulled into his driveway just in time to see Rick ushering Sam into the house. It had snowed again, and a light layer of powder covered the front lawn, which Blake trudged through on his way to the door. Inside, he found Sam sitting on the living room couch, gray eyes distant and face expressionless.

"Well, what did she tell you?" he burst out, his boots bringing a pile of snow onto the thick carpet. He didn't care about the wet stains beneath his feet. All he cared about was getting a break in this damn case.

"Nothing." Sam's voice sounded hollow, devoid of any emotion. She'd removed the glasses and wig, and though her natural honey-brown hair fell down her shoulders in loose waves, the makeup altering her features made her look like a stranger.

"She wouldn't talk?" Disappointment erupted in his chest.

"She wouldn't be pressured," Sam corrected.

Their gazes collided, and for one brief second, he saw

defiance in those gray circles. Almost as if she viewed him as the enemy now.

"Gentle coaxing and pressure are two different things," he pointed out, sitting on an armchair and removing his boots. He stood, then bit back a curse when his sock connected with the wet snow he'd brought in. Great.

"She needs time," Sam returned.

"We don't have time. This guy could be grabbing another woman as we speak. We have no clue what triggers him, why he decides to go out and commit murder."

Sam remained firm. "She's not ready to talk about what happened. She needs to trust me first."

The implication settled in the pit of Blake's stomach like a fifty-pound weight.

"Forget it," he said flatly. "You're not going back."

Sam stood up and marched past him, stealing through the doorway and heading for the stairs. "I'm seeing her again tomorrow," she called over her shoulder.

A shot of anger rocketed through him. He stormed after her, intercepting her before she could climb the first step. With his arms crossed over his chest, he shot her a menacing look. "I won't allow it."

"You don't have any say in this, Blake."

It was the first time she'd said his name out loud, and the way it slipped from her lush mouth sent another shock wave through him. Desire this time, and it went straight to his groin.

"The hell I don't," he shot back, ignoring his arousal.

Her eyes, empty before, now flashed with unrestrained rebellion. "She needs me. I'm going back. End of story."

"For Christ's sake, are you looking to get yourself killed? Wasn't one near-death experience enough for you?"

Her jaw hardened. Shoving him aside, she charged up the

stairs and disappeared into the second-floor hallway. A few seconds later, a door slammed.

"Real tactful." Rick's dry voice broke the silence.

Blake turned to face his partner, who'd appeared in the doorway. "She can't go back there."

"She shouldn't," Rick corrected. He shook his head. "But she can if she chooses to. And after your superb way of handling that, I'm guessing she will."

Frustration boiled inside him, swirling in his stomach like a cluster of hornets until he clenched his fists to control himself. Goddamn it. It had been enough of a risk bringing Sam back to Chicago, taking her to a public place where anyone—including the killer—might recognize her. But letting her stay? Even for another hour, another day? That was a much bigger risk.

Blake shook his head. The damn file had never said how stubborn this woman was. Or fiery. Or shockingly sexy when she was angry. He'd always liked sassy women, the ones who never backed down from a challenge and didn't mind throwing a few challenges of their own.

Kate had been like that—stubborn, determined, so much so that she'd convinced him to take her to the warehouse that night. The night she'd been killed.

A vise of pain swiftly tightened over his chest.

Well, this time *he* would be the stubborn one. This situation didn't allow room for challenges. Or mistakes. Or putting the life of a woman he was really starting to like in danger.

"I'll call Knight. Maybe he can talk some sense into her, try and stop her," Blake muttered.

Rick snorted. "I doubt even a bulldozer could stop her."

Sam paced the small bedroom, fighting a losing battle in her mind. She wanted to call Beau. Wanted to hear her brother's voice and have him tell her that she was making the right decision by staying. Wanted to forget Blake's harsh comment and assure herself that Elaine Woodman needed her.

Calling Beau, however, wouldn't help any. He'd only tell her the FBI agent was right and she should leave the city. And forgetting Blake's remark wouldn't work, either, considering that she was well aware of the danger she'd be putting herself in if she stayed.

But could she really go? When she'd left Elaine's room earlier, she'd known in her heart that she couldn't possibly turn tail and run without getting through to the girl. Elaine was scarred. Physically. Emotionally. She'd told Sam she didn't have any family, just a mother who'd passed away years before and a father who'd run out on them long before. The loneliness in the girl's voice had struck a chord of sorrow in her. She couldn't let Elaine lie there in that bed day in and day out, couldn't let her drown in the pain, lose herself in anguished memories.

To hell with Blake and the FBI. She needed to do this. For the first time in months, she actually felt useful. Needed. She was tired of hiding away in that empty farmhouse, carrying around a shotgun and bursting into tears at any unfamiliar sound. What kind of life was that? What did that say about her? That she was a coward instead of a fighter?

She should've come back here a long time ago. Declined the new identity the FBI had given her, let the man who'd attacked her know she was alive and *dared* him to come find her. But she hadn't been strong enough then. The wounds had been too fresh.

She reached into her overnight bag for the T-shirt she'd brought to sleep in. She wasn't hiding anymore.

With the determined set of her jaw, she changed into her

nightshirt and headed for the bathroom to wash the makeup from her face and brush her teeth. It wasn't until she'd slid under the soft covers that she realized she hadn't eaten a thing since leaving Wellstock this afternoon. Somehow, the hunger had gone unnoticed all night. Seeing Elaine had been too big a distraction, but her growling stomach refused to be ignored any longer.

Sighing, she got out of bed and rolled a pair of heavy wool socks onto her bare feet. Then she left the room and headed downstairs, wondering if Blake was still awake.

"Hungry?"

Yep, he was awake. Sam nearly tripped over her own feet as she spotted him in the hall. He'd changed into a pair of black sweatpants and a snug black T-shirt, and in the dark clothing he blended into the shadows. Taking a step toward her, he offered a tentative smile.

"Starved," she finally admitted.

He followed her into the kitchen and flicked on the light, bathing the large space in a yellow glow. Sam glanced at the black marble counter and shiny silver appliances, getting the impression that not much cooking went on in this room. The thin layer of dust on the stove confirmed her suspicions.

"Have a seat." He gestured to one of the stools at the counter. "I'll fix you something. Do you like roast beef?"

"Yep."

Blake kept his back to her as he opened the fridge and pulled out various items. He walked over to the pantry and removed a loaf of bread, then, back still turned, began preparing her a sandwich.

She was startled when he finally spoke. "I'm sorry about what I said." Slowly, he turned to meet her gaze. Regret shone in his deep brown eyes.

"It's all right."

"No." He took a breath. "I shouldn't have made light of what you went through. So please accept my apology."

"Apology accepted."

With a nod, he returned his attention to preparing her food, and a few moments later dropped a plate holding a thick roast-beef sandwich in front of her. "Want a glass of milk?" he offered.

"Sure."

He poured milk into a tall glass and handed it to her, then leaned against the sink as she ate. "Are you serious about visiting Elaine again?"

She chewed slowly, seeing the worry on his face and wondering why she wanted so badly to reassure him. He was the one who was supposed to tell her that everything would be okay, not the other way around.

"I have to," she said after swallowing. "I...I connected with her, Blake. I only spoke to her for a half hour, but for some reason I feel as if I need to, I don't know, help her...." She searched for the right words. "Heal her."

She quickly polished off the rest of the sandwich and then gulped down her milk. Blake just watched as she rinsed off the plate and glass, and dried her hands with a flower-patterned dish towel. When she glanced over at him, his face had an unreadable expression that made her forehead wrinkle. Was he angry with her? He'd sure been pissed off earlier when she'd informed him that she wasn't going anywhere, and yet you'd think he'd be happy about her decision. He'd been chasing this killer so long he had to be getting desperate, had to be anxious to catch him.

That her decision to stay upset him only told Sam that Blake Corwin was a good man. He wouldn't risk her life, even if it meant letting the Rose Killer get away.

And sure, she didn't want to risk her life, either, but what other option did she have? To place women like Elaine Woodman in jeopardy? She knew the burden didn't need to fall solely on her shoulders, but she still felt she needed to contribute to the investigation. If only to gain her own sense of closure.

"What did you talk to Elaine about?" Blake's quiet, husky voice broke through the brief silence. He moved over to the stool she'd just occupied and sat down, resting his powerful arms on the counter. Watching her.

Her gaze flitted to his strong biceps. A part of her, a long-buried part, wondered how it would feel to be encircled by those big arms. How did he hold a woman? Gently, like she was a fragile piece of china? Or would his embrace be passionate, solid and unyielding, a man claiming the woman in his arms as his own?

She bit her lower lip, disturbed by her thoughts. Absently she leaned against the counter and murmured, "Fear. We talked a lot about fear."

"Hers or yours?"

"Both." She exhaled shakily. "I showed her my scars." Though Blake's gaze remained on her face, she was still compelled to press her wrists to her sides, shielding the scars from him. "And then she…" Her voice finally broke.

"Then she what?" Blake stood up and closed the distance between them. She thought he might reach out and touch her but he didn't. Just stood in front of her, somber as always.

"She took off her hospital gown and showed me her bandages." She lifted her head, searched his face imploringly. "There were so many bandages, Blake. Why would he do that to her? Why didn't he do that to me?"

A wave of dizziness swept over her as she remembered all that white gauze on Elaine's body. On her chest. Her breasts.

Her legs. The horror Sam hadn't let herself reveal then slammed into her now, making her knees wobble and her hands tremble violently. She didn't even realize that she was crying until Blake drew her into his arms and she noticed her tears staining his shirt.

He held her tightly, and her earlier unspoken question was answered. His grip was gentle. But solid.

She pressed her face against the crook of his neck and cried, wondering why she wasn't pulling back. She wasn't supposed to feel sheltered in this man's arms. In any man's arms.

She was supposed to be terrified by a simple touch, panicked by a mere look, but Blake's touches, Blake's looks, evoked none of that in her. They only brought warmth.

And desire.

"Don't cry," he murmured, running a large hand over her shoulder blades. "I promised you it would be all right, re-member?"

She inched back, not breaking their contact, but not sinking into it, either. "How can it be, when he's still out there?"

A lone tear slid down her cheek, but Blake brushed it away with his thumb before she could lift her hand. "I'm going to find him, Sam. I'm going to stop him, and that's not a promise—it's a guarantee."

His certainty hung in the air. He sounded so relentlessly convincing that she actually believed him.

She tilted her head and saw his determined brown eyes, the firm set of his wide mouth, and as their gazes locked, the air in the kitchen swiftly changed. It hissed and sizzled, crackled like twigs under the sneakers of a morning jogger. She wanted to look away, to walk away, to make it stop, but she stood frozen in place. Waiting. Waiting for what?

Unable to take her eyes off his mouth, Sam just watched

as he leaned closer and closer, knowing what was about to happen and not doing a thing to stop it. She stared at his lips, saw them part, saw his pulse throbbing in his throat.

Closer that gorgeous mouth came, and suddenly it was brushing over hers in the lightest of kisses.

A tiny gasp tore from her throat, but he covered it with his lips and swallowed it with his kiss. A gentle kiss, the soft brush of his lips against hers, the teasing flick of his tongue. The spicy, masculine scent of him suffused her senses, making her woozy with desire. The fervor of her response stunned her. Her tongue greedily darted out to taste him. Her breasts eagerly rubbed against the hardness of his chest. Her entire body was overcome with sweet warmth. Nothing had ever felt as good as Blake Corwin's kiss. And yet it was a controlled kiss, one that told her he was the type of man who'd never fully let down his guard, never succumb to the pleasures of the flesh before clearing it with his head.

She wasn't sure if it was that disturbing notion that made her pull back, or if it was the unfamiliar quickening of her pulse and the loud gallop of her heart. Whatever it was, she broke the kiss, stumbling back and watching him warily.

The flush of his face, the lust-filled, slightly glazed look of his eyes, showed that he'd lost at least some control. He looked startled, blinking as if emerging from a hazy dream. As if he couldn't quite believe what he'd done.

His hands promptly dropped from her waist, but not before she felt them trembling. With a soft curse, he shook his head as if he were trying to shake the bewilderment from it. His voice was hoarse as he uttered, "I'm sorry."

Chapter 5

Sam swallowed. Tried to make sense of what had just happened. Was *she* sorry?

It quickly dawned on her that she wasn't.

Dammit, why not? Though she'd been the one to pull away, she found herself wanting to kiss him again, to taste his firm lips and lose herself in his powerful arms again.

Not a soothing realization, not for a woman who'd months ago—days ago—cringed at the mere thought of having a man touch her. The attack had broken something inside her. Her trust, her faith, her ability to ever feel safe around a man. Yet here she was, staring at the rueful face of the man who'd just kissed her, and she not only felt protected but more turned on than ever.

"I mean it, Sam. I'm sorry," he said when she didn't reply.

She walked around the counter, wanting to put some distance between them as she absorbed the strange emotions swirling through her. "It's all right." She was shocked that she could keep her voice so steady when her pulse still wasn't.

His jaw tight, Blake rubbed his temples. "I shouldn't have done that."

The shame in his tone irritated her. "I had a part in it too, you know."

"*I* kissed you."

"I *let* you."

He let out a strangled groan. "I took advantage of a vulnerable moment."

He turned around and pressed his clenched fists on the edge of the sink. Shoulders stiff. Back wrought with tension.

She averted her eyes. She didn't want to see that look of shame still swimming in his eyes, not when she was feeling the furthest thing from ashamed. If anything, she suddenly felt liberated. For the first time in six months she'd let a man get close to her. Whether she fully trusted Blake Corwin she didn't know, but the very fact that he'd been able to get within two feet of her, that she'd allowed him to kiss her, at least hinted that she was learning to trust again.

"Sam, look at me." His pained voice made her glance up. When she did, she saw that his control was back, that cool steady composure she'd begun to suspect was his trademark. "You're probably the most beautiful woman I've ever met."

Huh?

She would've said *thank you* if it weren't so damn obvious that there was a *but* coming.

"And—I'm attracted to you."

She blinked in surprise. "You are?"

"Were you not here for that kiss?" he grumbled.

A small laugh slid out of her throat. "Were you not here

for what happened *after* the kiss? Your bumbling apology and that spiel about taking advantage of me?"

A flicker of amusement filled his gaze, but it faded fast. "Look, I won't deny the attraction, but—" and there it was "—I also won't act on it again." He slowly unclenched his fists and let his hands dangle at his side. Master of control.

She lifted a curious brow. "Why not?"

"Because I'm in the middle of a case."

"Isn't that your job, to work cases?"

"Yeah."

He was looking at her like she was a complete idiot, so she tried to rephrase. "I mean, you must work a lot of cases a year, probably one after the other, right?"

Blake's eyes grew wary. "Yes."

"So if you don't get romantically involved with anyone while you're on a case, and if you're always on a case, then when *do* you get romantically involved?"

He offered a faint smile. "Is that some kind of riddle?"

"It's a valid question," she said in her defense. "When do you make time for your personal life?"

"I don't," he said simply.

"You don't?" she echoed, dubious.

He cast what looked like a self-deprecating smile her way. "I don't do relationships well," he admitted in a gruff voice. "Actually, I don't do them at all. Not anymore."

"What happened to make you decide that?"

"I lost the woman I was going to marry."

Since she hadn't really been expecting an answer, his candor thoroughly surprised her.

Before she could open her mouth to press for more details, Blake reassumed his professional demeanor. "It's late. You should get some sleep."

"I'm not tir—"

"Listen, Sam, I don't agree with your decision to see Elaine again. But if you feel you need to, I'll do everything in my power to make sure that you are kept safe." He offered a brisk nod. "Good night."

Disbelief poured into her like a gush of water. She watched in stunned silence as Blake disappeared into the darkened hallway.

What on earth had just happened? One second he was kissing her, the next he was apologizing, and then he was gone. Just like that.

She sagged back against the counter, listening to the troubling sound of Blake's footsteps ascending the stairs. Her mouth still throbbed from his kiss and every muscle in her body was taut, coiled with anticipation that was obviously going to be left unsatisfied.

Why had he kissed her? Why had he stopped? And why had he told her about losing the woman he'd loved when it was clearly something he didn't like to talk about?

Rubbing her forehead, she tried to push the questions from her mind, knowing that, like her desire, they wouldn't be satisfied. And maybe that was for the best. Maybe she didn't want to know about Blake's lost love, or why he didn't feel he could get involved again. Maybe what she really needed to do was take his lead and focus on the only thing that mattered right now: catching the madman who'd attacked her and putting an end to his reign of terror.

And maybe—though this was a pretty big maybe—she might actually be able to go to bed without lying awake all night thinking about Blake's kiss.

When Sam walked into Elaine's hospital room early the next morning, she found the young woman in tears.

As heart-wrenching as that was, witnessing Elaine's obvious distress only made Sam glad that she hadn't listened to Blake's suggestion about saving this visit for tonight.

When she'd awakened, the very last thing she'd wanted to do was sit around Blake's house all day, twiddling her thumbs while she waited for night to fall so she could see Elaine. Blake had tried talking her out of it, but in the end she'd convinced him that the morning visit wouldn't be the end of the world. She hadn't been comfortable on her way up to Elaine's room, dodging nurses and visitors in the halls, but now she was happy that she hadn't listened to Blake's objections.

She wasted no time rushing to Elaine's side.

Without hesitation she pulled Elaine into her arms, gently stroked her brown hair, and murmured, "It's okay. Tell me what happened."

Elaine simply whimpered and clutched at the corner of the newspaper as if it were a lifeline she couldn't let go of.

Pulling back, Sam reached for the box of tissues on the bedside table and handed one to the young woman. "Please, Elaine. Tell me what's got you so upset."

Elaine wordlessly handed her the newspaper, which was open to the wedding announcements. The top of the page displayed a photograph of a young, smiling couple. The caption read *Charles and Davis to marry*.

Sam looked up, questioning. "Do you know him?" She glanced again at the handsome blond man in the picture. Matthew Charles.

"My ex-boyfriend." Elaine's voice was scarcely above a whisper. "We broke up a few months ago. It was before the…attack."

"And he's getting married. Is that why you're upset?"

Elaine sniffled. "I know I shouldn't be. After all, we broke up. But I never stopped loving him. I just needed to focus on my new job for a while. He didn't take it well, started dating another girl pretty soon afterward." Her gaze drifted to the attractive blonde in the photo. "I was thinking of calling him about a week before…the attack…but I was scared that he and his new girlfriend might be serious. I guess they were."

Sympathy bloomed in Sam's chest. Though she couldn't say she'd ever truly been in love, she did know what it was like to care deeply about someone. She could just imagine how Elaine felt now, dead to all who knew her, seeing a past love moving on with his life when she couldn't do the same.

"It's not as if I want him back." A bitter scowl creased Elaine's delicate mouth. "After what happened to me, I don't expect another man to ever want me."

Sam quickly cupped Elaine's chin and forced her to look at her. "Don't say that," she ordered. "You'll fall in love again."

"Who's going to love me?" Elaine laughed harshly and lowered the sheet covering her body. All that gauze instantly sent a piercing shot of pain to Sam's heart. "I'm damaged."

"You're not damaged." Sam's voice wavered. "I don't want to ever hear you say that."

It became hard for her to breathe, especially when the words coming out of this young woman's mouth were the exact words Sam had uttered not so long ago. *Nobody will ever want me. I'm tainted. I'm damaged goods.* That's what she'd told Annette Hanson, what she'd believed for months after the attack. Normal thoughts to have, she knew that. Being attacked and left for dead did that to a girl.

Elaine had every right to feel the way she did. Hard as it was to admit—and it made her guilty as hell even thinking it—Elaine had it worse than her. Sam had thought that one rose on her body, that stark evidence of being branded, would be enough to send any man running. But Elaine had a lot more scars. So many that Sam wondered if the girl would ever meet someone willing to look past the damaged shell and appreciate the courageous beauty inside.

"I wish I'd died that day," Elaine whispered. "Do you ever wish that?"

"I did at first," she admitted. "I was so angry, lying there in the hospital. I went back and forth from self-pity, thinking I was better off dead, to self-hatred, blaming myself for what happened."

"How could it have been your fault?"

"It wasn't." She smiled faintly. "But at the time, I thought it was. I left my bedroom window unlatched. That's how he got in."

"He attacked you in your house?"

Sam nodded. "I got back from a party, still in my slinky red dress, a little tipsy, too. I had no clue that anyone was in the house. No clue. But when I went up to my room—" she sucked in much-needed oxygen "—he was there. Waiting. He even said hello."

Her throat suddenly burned with vicious-tasting acid and she feared she might throw up. *Hello*. She could still hear that raspy male whisper, eerily calm in the darkness of her bedroom as he slid up behind her and reached a hand around to press a knife to her throat. Her first thought was that she was being robbed, and she remembered saying, "Take whatever you want. Just don't hurt me."

And he'd laughed.

"He. Laughed." She gritted her teeth so hard she feared she'd break her jaw. "He told me he didn't want my belongings, but that I'd pay. And the funny thing—" she chuckled callously "—I never thought to ask what I was paying for."

She heard Elaine sniffle again, and when she glanced over, she saw that the tears had returned. "He said that to me," the girl murmured, her face growing pale. "He told me I'd pay."

It took a second to realize that, for the first time, Elaine was talking about what had happened to her. That small detail made Sam forget all about her own pain, made her own tragedy take a back seat and reminded her why she was here.

"What else did he say?" she asked, trying not to push.

Elaine wiped the tears from her eyes. "He told me if I made a sound, he'd slit my throat. He had a knife, so I believed him." She paused. "I was in the underground parking lot of my office, about to go on my lunch break. A coworker had wanted to walk down with me, but I laughed and said Bob the security guard would kick anyone's butt if they tried to mess with me. Bob sits in the lot all day, making sure everything's okay." She shook her head, looking betrayed. "He wasn't there that day."

From the bare details Blake and Rick had provided, Sam knew that the security guard had been knocked unconscious and was out cold in his booth when Elaine had been taken.

"He came up behind me and told me to be a good girl, and then there was something over my mouth. A rag, and it smelled sweet." Elaine took a long breath. "That's all I remember in the garage. When I came to, I was blindfolded and gagged and my hands and feet were bound. I think he put me in the back of a van, but I don't remember seeing one in the parking garage."

"Did he talk to you at all?"

Elaine shook her head. "I heard the radio playing, but it was kind of muffled, like there was a partition or something. And I kept smelling…" She drifted off.

"What did you smell?"

"I'm not sure." Elaine bit her lower lip, confusion

marring her face. "Something fruity and flowery. I couldn't place it. I still can't. But sometimes when I wake up I think I smell it. It makes me sick." Her blue eyes flashed. "*He* makes me sick."

Without a word, Sam drew her into her arms, touching her soft brown hair and fighting back tears of her own. It broke her heart hearing the girl's anguished sobs, and when Elaine finally pulled back and rubbed her puffy red eyes, Sam knew it was time to go.

She couldn't ask Elaine to put herself through any more pain. There would be time to hear the rest of her story. She'd make time. Right now, she simply couldn't let another sliver of horror reach the surface. Not just for Elaine's sake. But for her own.

"Let's go," Blake said roughly when she stepped out of Elaine's room.

He took hold of her arm, and Sam allowed him to drag her away. No point resisting, not when he still looked displeased by her insistence on coming here this morning. He'd thank her later, though. The sparse details she'd gotten from Elaine in less than an hour were more than Blake, the FBI and the Chicago PD had managed to obtain in weeks.

"Would you ease up?" she muttered, staring at the white knuckles gripping her arm.

He slowly loosened his grasp but didn't slow down. She matched his strides, following him down the brightly lit corridor toward the stairwell. When she'd come here with Rick, they'd taken the service elevator but apparently Blake wasn't taking any chances. His route required them to walk down to the basement, which housed none other than the morgue.

God, she didn't look forward to going down there again like

she did the previous night, walking the creepy morgue hallways and listening to the fluorescent lights buzzing overhead.

It scared her to realize that six months ago she'd come pretty close to being another one of those bodies in the morgue.

Blake didn't say a word as he held open the door for her, but she didn't need to be a mind reader to know that he was angry. She wondered if he realized how sexy he looked when his eyes flashed like that, when his strong jaw jutted out impatiently. Not that she would ever let him know. If there was one thing she'd learned about men in her twenty-six years, it was that unnecessary strokes to their ego only inflated it.

He descended the steps so quickly she nearly stumbled forward trying to keep up with him. He quickly caught her arm to steady her, and heat sizzled right through the sleeve of her sweater where he'd touched her. She had to pause on the landing to catch her breath—Blake's spicy aftershave and intoxicating nearness were too much to handle.

She suddenly thought of Elaine's despair over her boyfriend's engagement, the look in her eyes when she'd wondered if anyone would fall in love with her again, and Sam couldn't help wondering if the same thing applied to her. Could someone fall in love with *her?* Could Blake?

He'd admitted to being attracted to her, but attraction was a far cry from love. Men knew how to separate the two, and none of the relationships she'd had in the past had ever transitioned from sex to love. The men she'd dated hadn't loved her. They'd loved the *idea* of her, the model who wore little bikinis and posed on some of the world's most beautiful beaches. They liked the glitz of her life, the glamour, and yes, the sex.

She couldn't remember the last time a man had shown interest in getting to know *her* and not the model.

"You okay?" Blake asked gruffly, jerking her from her unsettling thoughts.

She slowly nodded. "Yeah. I'm fine. Let's get out of here."

She took a step forward just as the door to the landing swung open and nearly knocked her over. Startled, she promptly dropped the purse that had been dangling loosely from her fingers. The contents spilled out onto the floor and both she and Blake dropped to their knees to collect the fallen items.

"Shoot, I'm sorry about that," came a male voice, and a moment later a third person was on his knees, a third set of hands grabbing at a tube of lipstick that was perilously close to rolling down the steps.

Sam glanced up to look at the man who'd startled her.

A nanosecond later she forced her head back down.

Beside her, Blake shifted over and leaned forward, trying to shield her from the reporter who was currently sharing the small space with them.

The man wore his press credentials around his neck, and he had that hungry look in his eyes that most members of the media around there sported. Cindy Wilcox, who was married to the latest Hollywood action hero, had apparently gone into labor, and the reporters lurking in the hospital were eager to outscoop each other. No doubt this man—Wayne Reynolds, his ID read—was trying to find a way to sneak onto the obstetrics ward.

Although she felt fairly concealed in the blond wig, thick glasses and well-applied makeup, Sam's heart raced like a thoroughbred galloping to the finish line. She began clawing at the items that didn't even belong to her. A small pack of tissues. A brown leather wallet. Breath mints.

The reporter wouldn't leave. His gaze was now glued to her face. She could sense his eyes on her, and the intrusion made her feel like a wild animal trapped by greedy poachers. She needed to get out of here. Right. Now.

"Hey, do I know you from somewhere?" Wayne Reynolds suddenly asked.

Blake's entire body went taut the second the question came out of the reporter's mouth. He leaned closer to Sam, trying to appear casual, which was extremely difficult to do when Reynolds' eyes were sweeping over Sam's face.

A vulture circling its prey.

"I doubt it." Blake spoke in a low, noncommittal voice. He swiped at the last item on the floor and shoved it into the purse, then hauled Sam to her feet. "Lorraine and I just moved here from California."

Blake kept her in front of him as they moved toward the stairs, shielding her from the nosy reporter, but Reynolds trailed after them, taking the steps two at a time so that he was already there at the next landing when they came down.

Reynolds squinted at Sam. "You seem *really* familiar."

"I guess I have that kind of face," she managed.

Blake noticed she was trying to tone down her normally husky voice, and he wished she wouldn't speak altogether. A protective lump lodged in his throat when he saw that her hands were shaking so hard she had to press them to her sides. He understood her fear; she'd been hiding away for six months precisely to avoid something like this from happening, and in less than six minutes that feeling of security had been ripped away from her.

Damn it. Why had he let her talk him into bringing her back to the hospital?

"Listen, buddy, my wife and I need to be somewhere," Blake said coolly. With an equally cool smile, he planted a hand on the reporter's shoulder and effectively moved

Reynolds out of their path. He glanced at Sam. "Come on, sweetheart."

She nodded meekly, then took a step forward. As she walked, she pushed a few strands of synthetic blond hair away from her visibly pale face.

And that's when it happened.

The wig snagged on the wristband of Sam's thin silver watch. It didn't fall off, but it shifted, enough for the reporter watching her to get an eyeful of her natural brown hairline.

Blake's heart stopped.

Quickly, Sam adjusted the wig, but it was too late. The reporter's eyes had narrowed and he was stumbling across the landing.

Blake's arm tightened around Sam's shoulder. His body was so stiff he could barely will his legs to move. His pulse thudded loudly in his ears. He had to get her out of here. Now. As he urged her to continue down the stairs, Reynolds stayed hot on their heels. The other man caught up, grabbing Sam's wrist, trying to stop her so he could get a better look.

She tried to shrug his hand away but Blake beat her to it. He planted both his palms on Reynolds' meaty chest and gave the other man a shove. Gaze glittering with menace, Blake said, "Touch her again and I'm calling security."

Reynolds just stared. "It's her, isn't it?"

Blake resisted the urge to order Sam to run. As fast as she could. But he knew taking off in an Olympic sprint would only fuel Reynolds's suspicions.

The reporter's expression transformed into a strange glimmer, a mixture of doubtful and dumbfounded. "Samantha Dawson!" he exclaimed, almost out of breath.

"You're mistaken," Blake said in a voice that could freeze an ocean. "This is my wife, Lorraine."

And then he tightly gripped Sam's hand and practically dragged her down the stairs again, leaving the reporter stupefied.

Blake's legs could barely carry him as they made their escape. They finally reached the basement, where the white walls and fluorescent hospital lighting made his temples ache.

By the time they got outside, his heart was still thudding, and he felt so on edge he couldn't even formulate a sentence.

He didn't say a word as he shoved her into the passenger seat, rounded the SUV and got in. He careened away from the hospital at full speed, tires screeching and the smell of burnt rubber filling the car. From the corner of his eye he noticed how stunned Sam looked, how shaky her hands still were, but he couldn't bring himself to comfort her, or assure her that what just happened was no biggie.

Because it *was* big. It was *huge*.

And he was absolutely furious. At her, for stubbornly insisting she come back here. At himself, for letting her.

It was only when he came to a screeching halt in the driveway of his house that he turned to her, eyes flashing, unable to control the anger and fear bubbling in the pit of his stomach.

"So much for your brilliant idea to stay in town," he snapped.

Chapter 6

"Jesus, Corwin, you need to get her out of there." Michael Knight, the man known for his calm, unruffled manner, sounded absolutely livid. His deep baritone voice shot through the airwaves, piercing Blake's eardrums with its sheer volume.

Not that he blamed his boss for being furious. Blake was pretty damn enraged himself. He hadn't said a single word to Samantha since reprimanding her in the car, and yet again she'd retreated upstairs. But he wasn't about to apologize for what he'd said. He didn't blame her for being recognized by the meddlesome reporter, but he sure as hell blamed her for putting herself in the position to be recognized.

"At least he didn't get a photo," he said in a stab at sounding optimistic.

"He doesn't need one." Knight cursed loudly. "One of the men here did some checking on Reynolds. Guess who he works for? FOX News. That's right, home of Geraldo Rivera."

Blake closed his eyes.

"The CPD and the Chicago field office have been dealing with calls from reporters for the last hour. Reporters demanding to know if Samantha Dawson's death had been staged and if she's officially come out of hiding to stop the Rose Killer."

Pain vibrated in his temples. Dammit. This wasn't good. Not good at all.

"How could you let this happen?" Knight roared. "That woman is a walking target. You were supposed to have her back in the safe house by now."

"She wouldn't leave."

"It was your job to make sure she did."

So much for being Knight's best agent. Recrimination coupled with a streak of protectiveness collided in his chest. He'd known that letting Sam stay in Chicago was a bad idea. Hell, he'd warned her that something like this could happen. Too bad the stubborn woman hadn't listened.

But he should have known better than to let himself get soft. He could have tried harder to make her leave, worked harder to talk some sense into her, but had he done that? Oh, no. One look at those gorgeous gray eyes and he'd been sucked in, ready to let Samantha Dawson do anything her sexy little heart desired.

"Where's Scott?" Knight demanded.

"On his way here."

"Good. Neither of you is to leave that woman's side until we can arrange for a new safe house out of state."

"Out of state? Why not take her back to Wellstock?"

"We're getting her out of Illinois, Corwin. It's too risky to keep her here with the media sniffing around."

His headache threatened to become a full-blown migraine. "She won't go."

"You'll make her go. I don't care if you have to cuff her to do it."

Knight had hung up. Biting back a string of four-letter words, Blake sank onto one of the wooden dining room chairs and buried his face in his hands.

Trouble. The woman was nothing but trouble. Did she not value her own life? Hadn't she realized that by putting her foot down and going to see Elaine Woodman again she'd be taking a tremendous risk? The sick bastard who'd almost murdered her was too smart to leave loose ends. If he learned that Sam was still alive, who was to say he wouldn't track her down and slit her throat this time?

Not her wrists, but her goddamn *throat*.

His chest ached at the thought. He'd only spent a few days with Sam, yet he knew that if anything happened to her, something inside him would be destroyed. He'd already lost the woman he was going to marry thanks to a man as twisted as the Rose Killer.

He'd never recover if he lost Sam, too.

He gulped. Hard. Frantically searched his mind, trying to figure out exactly when he'd become this attached to Samantha Dawson.

Was it before or after you kissed her? came the taunting voice in his head.

Christ. Not now. He didn't want to think about that kiss. He'd been pushing it out of his mind all day, and yet the memory continued sneaking right back in, like a dog eager to play fetch with its owner.

His groin tightened as swiftly as it had last night when he'd captured Sam's mouth with his. When the feel of her lush, moist lips had sent him into a state of arousal he'd never experienced before.

What the hell had he been thinking, kissing her? He'd known, the second he lowered his mouth to hers, that it was a bad idea. That it was *wrong*. And yet he couldn't seem to stop himself. It was like an out-of-body experience, as if his mouth and tongue and hands belonged to another man, a man who didn't seem to understand how inappropriate it was to kiss a goddamn *witness*.

He'd wanted to kick himself afterward. Actually, no. When he'd pulled back and caught sight of the arousal swimming in Sam's luminous gray eyes, he'd wanted to kiss her again. *Then* he'd wanted to kick himself.

If he hadn't managed to impose that sliver of control, he would've made love to her right then and there, peeled every layer of clothing from her body and laved his tongue over every inch of her perfect skin. That's why he'd walked away. To stop himself from adding another item to his how-I-screwed-up-today list. That, and because he wasn't sure he could control himself if he kissed her again.

Sam was too vulnerable. He would never take advantage of her, but he got the feeling that she wouldn't mind if he did. Which meant one of them needed to remain in control, and it obviously had to be him.

"Knight's not happy," Rick said grimly as he strode into the dining room.

Blake swallowed back myriad emotions clinging to his throat. Business. That's what he needed to focus on now. "I'm not too happy, either," he replied. "That reporter knew who she was."

Rick joined him at the table. "Do you think he noticed what floor you'd come from? Think he's smart enough to sneak into the ICU to do some investigating?"

"Let's hope not."

Rick swore. "We need to get Elaine out of there. Her doctor was going to discharge her in a few days, but we've got to speed up the process. She can't stay there a second longer."

"I know."

"I'll call Mel and tell her to start making arrangements."

The sound of timid footsteps caused Blake to turn his head. Gray eyes lined with remorse, Sam stood in the doorway. She'd scrubbed off her makeup, and gone were the wig and glasses. Her long caramel-colored hair fell over her shoulders in careless waves, resting just above the scooped neckline of the long-sleeved green sweater she'd changed into. A pair of faded jeans encased her long legs, emphasizing her shapely thighs and were rolled up at the bottom to reveal her pale, slender ankles.

She was so damn pretty. Just looking at her made his body ache.

"I'm sorry." Her quiet voice broke through his troubled thoughts.

He watched as she entered the room and settled in the chair next to Rick's. She wrung her hands together, looking unhappy, and for a moment he almost regretted snapping at her earlier.

Almost.

Pushing away the tender sympathy threatening to seep into his chest, Blake shot her a firm look. "It's too late for apologies. Your time's up, Samantha. We're getting you out of here tonight."

Desperation flickered in her gaze. "Will you let me say goodbye to Elaine?"

"No."

"But… Dammit, Blake! She'll think I abandoned her."

"She'll understand."

Rick broke the exchange by turning to Sam and asking, "Did she tell you anything useful today?"

Sam appeared reluctant as she tore her gaze from Blake's. "Actually, she did."

She quickly related the details she'd learned about the abduction and the scent Elaine had described, then excused herself. Blake heard her moving around in the kitchen, glad she hadn't argued any further about leaving the city. This time, they would do things his way, and his way required getting Sam out of Dodge before anything worse happened.

"It'll be hard to find the vehicle," Rick said, rubbing his chin. "There are probably a million vans in the city. Going through DMV records would be pointless, considering we don't have a license plate number, not to mention the guy's name."

Blake chewed on the inside of his cheek, trying to bring into focus the idea nagging at the back of his mind. He knew the chances of finding the van weren't good, so instead he mulled over the other details Sam had provided. The scent Elaine had mentioned. Something fruity… Was their guy a fruit wholesaler? A grocer?

Naah, that didn't sit right with him. Fruity and flowery. Flowery. Flowers.

Flowers.

Christ, how had he overlooked it? Flowers. No. *Roses.*

The puzzle pieces in Blake's head slid into place. He wanted to slap himself for missing the connection, but up until now, they hadn't had much to go on. The first three victims were dead. Sam was attacked in her home. But Elaine had been different from the start, the only woman who'd been transported to another location. Thank God she'd remembered such a vital scent. Flowers. The guy carved roses into his victims' skin, for God's sake. It wouldn't be a stretch believing his line of work had something to do with the damn things.

He sat up straight and slammed his hand down. The

sound of his palm slapping on the smooth dining room table echoed through the room. "He's a goddamn florist," he said with a groan.

At that moment Sam reappeared in the doorway with a steaming cup of coffee in her hands. Her eyes widened at his declaration. "Roses," she exclaimed. "Elaine smelled roses in that van!"

Looking excited, she returned to her seat and set down her mug. Blake wanted to ask her to leave, let him and Rick deal with this investigation without civilian involvement, but the enthusiasm sparkling in her eyes made him reconsider. She looked energized, hopeful, and he couldn't bring himself to send her away as if she were some disobedient child who shouldn't be talking to the grown-ups.

"That's what you're thinking, isn't it?" she demanded.

"It makes sense," he answered, still brooding over the notion. "A florist. Landscaper maybe. Gardener. Delivery guy. Whatever it is, I'm convinced the bastard works with flowers."

"Which," Rick said, "could explain why Diana, Candace and Roberta opened their doors to him. If he's a deliveryman, showing up with flowers, they wouldn't be suspicious."

"Candace and Roberta?" Sam echoed.

"The first two victims," Rick explained.

"They let him in? Willingly?"

"Seems so," Rick confirmed. "There was no sign of forced entry in their homes, which led the police to believe that the guy somehow coaxed his way inside."

"Why didn't we think of this before?" Blake said with chagrin. "The profilers at Quantico came up with a list of people someone might let into their home. Plumber, cable guy, Avon lady. How did they miss flower-delivery guy?"

"As I recall, the profilers believed the roses were more

symbolic. They didn't associate it with his occupation." Rick shrugged. "And to be fair, most people just sign for flowers at their doorstep. Not many deliverymen offer to come in and arrange the damn things."

"But this one did."

Sam intervened. "We could be wrong about this, you know. It's just speculation."

"It's the first thing in this case that makes sense," Blake corrected.

"But we didn't find flowers in any of their homes," Rick spoke with a troubled frown. "Forensics combed the houses for trace evidence and came up empty-handed. If our guy showed up at their doors with a bouquet, he must have taken it back with him."

"Not to raise the suspicions of the cops?" Sam offered. She leaned forward. "Most of the victims were married, or were living with someone, right? If their significant other came home and saw a floral arrangement that wasn't there before, he'd tell the cops about it."

Blake nodded, and for a moment he experienced a flicker of deep respect for the brunette in front of him. She didn't need to be here, to listen to details about the man who'd tried to kill her, but not only was she calm and composed, she was offering real insight. He wondered if she realized her own strength.

Then he wondered if there was *anything* about this woman that didn't impress him so damn much.

"What about you?" Rick suddenly asked, staring at Sam. "Did you receive any flowers the day of the attack?"

A frown creased her forehead. "The day of? No. But…" She started biting on her bottom lip in a cute way that made Blake's mouth tingle. "A week before, I received a floral arrangement from a designer. I remember because I threw it in the trash the morning of the attack. I'd forgotten to put the flowers in water and they were a big dried-up mess by then."

"Do you remember what the delivery guy looked like?"

She scrunched up her face, deep in thought, then released a sigh. "Honestly? No. I wasn't paying much attention, just signed for the delivery and forgot all about it. I know it was a man, though."

"And you're sure the arrangement came a week before the attack?" Rick asked. He swiped Sam's mug and took a hearty sip, a sign that he was definitely getting keyed up. Whenever Rick got excited, he had the annoying tendency to snatch other people's drinks.

Sam didn't seem to mind, though. Instead she nodded in response to his question. "Yeah, it was definitely about a week before."

Rick glanced at Blake. "Goes against the profile."

Sam looked from one man to the other. "What do you mean?"

"The impression our profiler got is that the perp is a heat-of-the-moment kind of guy," Blake explained. "No evidence of stalking, no scouting out the victim's home beforehand. He seems to show up—maybe to deliver flowers—and then he snaps. We don't know why, but something seems to set him off."

"But in your case," Rick added, "if you're remembering the dates right, it would seem he waited a week before acting. Maybe he didn't want you to recognize him as the delivery guy from the prior week." He pulled out his notepad. "You said the flowers were sent by a designer?"

Sam nodded.

"Okay, then it should be easy to find out where the flowers came from. What was the designer's name?"

"Angelo D'Alessio. He sent the arrangement to thank me."

Something yanked at Blake's insides. Was that jealousy?

Whatever the annoying feeling was, he couldn't help but ask, "Thank you for what?"

Sam's cheeks turned a rosy shade of pink. "I modeled the final piece of his collection, a diamond-studded G-string. I don't usually do runway work, but he's a friend and I owed him a favor."

The word *G-string* coming out of Sam's sexy mouth was enough to set him on edge.

Next to him, Rick coughed. Blake suffered another jealous pang when he realized that Rick had probably been picturing the same thing.

Samantha Dawson wearing nothing but a G-string below her waist.

He willed away his arousal and forced his brain back to the northern region of his body. "Okay, so we'll compile a list of florists and people in related fields. This week we're meeting with the task force, so—"

The ring of his cell phone cut him off. Glancing at the caller ID, he suppressed a groan. Knight. This couldn't be good, his boss calling back so soon.

He picked up the phone, somewhat reluctant. "Corwin," he said in lieu of a greeting.

"Turn your television to FOX. Now." Knight hung up before Blake could open his mouth.

With a sigh, he rose from his seat and gestured for Rick and Sam to follow him into the living room. He grabbed the remote control from the coffee table and flicked on the set.

"Samantha Dawson, one of the highest-paid swimsuit models in the business, is alive." Wayne Reynolds's irritating voice filled the living room, making Blake curse out loud.

Holding a microphone, the reporter stood in front of Chicago General looking like the cat who'd just swallowed the biggest canary in the flock. The screen split to show Vanessa Highland, a FOX anchor. Addressing her correspondent in the field, Vanessa asked, "Are you sure about this, Wayne?"

"Yes, Vanessa. I just received confirmation from the funeral home that supposedly cremated Dawson's body. One of the staff members there confessed that the body had never been brought to the home. He suspected all along she was still alive."

"I'll have that jerk fired," Blake muttered.

"As you know, Vanessa, Dawson was attacked by the man the media dubbed the Rose Killer, who is still at large. The Rose Killer has already taken the lives of four women and Dawson was believed to be his fourth victim. Apparently, she survived the assault and was placed in protective custody by law enforcement."

"For her own safety, Wayne?"

"Yes. My source in the Chicago Police Department informed me that the Rose Killer is a very sick, very dangerous individual."

"No kidding," Rick spat out.

"And Vanessa, although Police Superintendent Jake Fantana denies that any of the victims were sexually assaulted, we believe rape is a likely component."

A soft gasp tore out of Sam's throat. From the corner of his eye, Blake saw her sag against Rick's arm.

"Wayne, why would Samantha Dawson come out of hiding, now of all times?"

"It could be related to the fact that Cindy Wilcox has been admitted to the hospital for complications with her pregnancy. My sources tell me that Dawson and action-star Bruce Wilcox's wife are very close. We believe Dawson decided to risk her own life to be with her dear friend at this difficult time."

Blake pressed a button on the remote and with a loud

crackle the screen went black. He turned slowly, not bothering to fill the devastating silence hanging over the room. He noticed that Sam's entire face had gone pale, as white as the snow covering the lawn. She trembled visibly, no longer holding on to Rick's arm but obviously swaying on her feet.

"My dear friend?" she finally burst out. "I don't even know Cindy Wilcox! And…sexual assault?" Disbelief turned to horror. "How could he…why would he…"

With a strangled sob, she spun on her heel and ran out of the room.

Sam was halfway up the stairs when she realized that she was acting hysterical. Sagging against the wall, she forced herself to breathe. Inhale. Exhale. *Focus. Don't let it tear you apart.* The calming voice whispering inside her head was absolutely right. She wouldn't fall apart. Wouldn't let the tactless words of an overly ambitious reporter get to her. Nor would she give in to the irrational urge telling her to blame Blake and the FBI for that news report.

As her ragged breaths steadied and her heartbeat slowed to its regular pace, she walked back down the stairs and headed into the hall bathroom, where she washed her tear-streaked face over the small, porcelain sink. She wasn't going to freak out or place blame on anyone. If anyone was to blame, it was her. Wasn't she the one who had refused to leave the city? Real smart on her part.

She dried her face with the soft towel hanging next to the sink. Then she sank down onto the closed toilet seat and forced herself to continue breathing normally. A minute passed. Two. Three. With each carefully measured breath, she released the panic that had lodged inside her chest. There. She'd had her moment of weakness. It was time to move on.

It gave her a sense of liberation, being able to even think those words. Moving on. For so long she'd crawled inside herself, tried to pretend the attack never happened. Didn't fight back, couldn't find the strength to do so.

Well, she'd found that strength now.

"Sam?"

She stepped out of the washroom and found Blake in the hallway. Hesitation lined his handsome features.

"Are you okay?" His tone revealed both worry and sympathy. The former touched her, the latter only grated. She didn't need his sympathy. She might have broken down in front of him and Rick, but her hysteria was done now.

"I'm fine. Really," she assured, catching his skeptical expression.

"You don't have to pretend with me." He looked reluctant, but finally stepped closer, looking as if he wanted to pull her into his arms. A crack in that iron control of his?

"I'm not pretending." She met his gaze head-on, unwavering. "That news segment upset me, but I got over it. No sense letting a bunch of lies tear me apart."

"All right." He cleared his throat. "Rick and I need to speak with you."

She nodded. Blake's gaze held hers for a moment, soft, concerned. Then he swallowed, his Adam's apple bobbing, and took a step back.

He moved toward the dining room, but before he reached the doorway the words she hadn't even known she'd wanted to say slipped out.

"He didn't rape me, Blake."

Slowly, their eyes connected again. She didn't falter, didn't look away, just held her head high and waited.

"I know," he finally said.

* * *

She was alive.

Alive.

That goddamn woman had fooled him.

"Keep us posted, Wayne." Vanessa Highland turned her snooty little face to the camera. "In case you're just tuning in now, we have received a report that Samantha Dawson, a rising star in the modeling world, is alive. Dawson was believed to be the fourth victim of the man the media has dubbed the Rose Killer…"

With a strangled groan, he jammed his finger on the remote control. The image on the outdated black-and-white television crackled, disappeared. It left an empty screen and a deafening silence that caused his entire body to shake.

Flames of rage led a fiery trail to his gut. His insides burned. Each breath came out ragged, punctuated with the hiss of betrayal.

He charged out of the musty back room, emerging into the space crammed to capacity with the roses he'd been surrounded with all his life. The scent of the flowers prickled his nostrils, made him nauseous, dizzy. As a child he'd loathed those roses. They'd been his father's obsession, and he'd grown up with the revolting knowledge that his only living relative loved a bunch of useless plants more than his own son.

And then he'd come home from the Gulf and suddenly those goddamn useless plants were all he had left. The obsession was now his.

He stared at the shears resting on the edge of one of the concrete planters, wanting to grab them, wanting to direct his rage toward the rows of flowers surrounding him like a pack of hungry wolves.

The uncharacteristic urge to destroy his prized possessions

escalated his fury. No. The roses were not to blame. The woman was to blame.

He'd known her true identity from the second he'd seen her in the *pornography* she passed off as high fashion. She wasn't like the others. She wasn't a pathetic facsimile of the woman he'd vowed to punish. She *was* that woman.

That's why he'd waited for her. He'd spent a week imagining how magnificent it would feel to get his hands on her, and when the time finally came, the satisfaction had been greater than anything he'd ever experienced. He'd left the house that night knowing he'd achieved the ultimate revenge, and yet something inside him had continued to burn. So he'd taken the other girl, dragged her to that warehouse and punished her until he couldn't see straight.

It hadn't been enough. The satisfaction never came. And now he knew why. Because the prey he was sure he'd punished still roamed free. Breathing. Mocking him.

She'd come back from the grave to taunt him. She had come back to hurt him again, to play with his mind and flaunt her treachery.

He eyed the shears again, fingers tingling with the urge to tear each plump rose from its stem and squash the petals beneath his boots.

No. *No.* His fury belonged elsewhere. He would save it for the woman who called herself Samantha Dawson.

Chapter 7

Rick was already seated at the dining room table when Sam and Blake walked in, drumming his fingers against the wood. He glanced up as they entered, then exchanged a look with Blake.

"What's going on?" Sam said carefully. Wariness climbed up her chest like a vine, coiling into a lump in the back of her throat. "Why do you two look so serious?"

Blake gestured for her to sit, and she did. Sinking into the chair next to her, he raked his fingers through his dark hair. "It's time for you to go, Sam."

She'd expected this, and yet the words brought a tug of desperation to her stomach. Seeing that reporter spin her pain and sensationalize her ordeal had been tough, but it only reinforced her conviction that she needed to see this through to the end.

If the Rose Killer suspected that she was alive, he might question the well-being of his latest victim. What if he learned that Elaine hadn't died the night he'd left her in the warehouse? What if he came after Elaine again?

That thought sent an avalanche of rage surging through Sam's body. She genuinely cared for the young woman, she wanted to help her, and running away again wouldn't achieve a solitary thing. Elaine still needed her, whether Blake and the FBI liked it or not, and Sam couldn't desert her. Not now.

"No," she found herself responding, her voice thick with emotion.

Blake released a sigh, as if he'd expected her to be difficult. "You don't have a choice. While you were in the bathroom, three other networks aired the story of your survival. The press is already camped out in front of police headquarters and outside the FBI field office here in the city. It's too risky for you to stay."

She tightened her lips. "Elaine needs me."

"Elaine is being moved to a safe house in Indiana. Tonight." Blake's normally rough voice softened. "You wouldn't be able to see her, even if you stayed."

"Will I be able to speak to her on the phone?"

"No. I mean, it could be arranged but—"

"Then arrange it."

"Sam—"

"I'm not leaving." She crossed her arms over her chest, tightly, desperately. "I can't leave. I *won't* leave." Blake opened his mouth but she silenced him with a glare. "And don't you dare tell me I don't have a choice. I *do* have a choice, Blake. The Bureau can't force me to go into hiding."

Neither agent answered, confirming that her words were correct.

"I won't leave," she repeated, a sliver of stubbornness slicing her tone.

"You'll be safer in Florida," Rick said quietly.

"Florida? That's where you want to ship me off to?" She snorted. "What, so I can lie on a beach all day and pretend the bastard who tried to kill me isn't murdering other women? No, thank you. I have as much, if not more, invested in this. I want to be here when that maniac is caught."

In a flat voice, Blake said, "No."

Hot flames ignited her body. Why was he being so difficult about this? It wasn't as if she were saying she wanted to use herself as bait to catch the killer; she just wanted to be in the city when he was captured.

"This isn't your choice," she said in a steely tone.

"Like hell it isn't. I'll arrest you for obstruction of justice if that's what it takes."

Disbelief rocketed through her. "Excuse me?"

"You heard me."

Rick sighed. "Blake—"

She interrupted angrily. "Do it and I'll call a press conference telling the country how the FBI is bullying the only witness they've got!"

"Sam—" Rick began.

"I need a moment alone with her, Rick," Blake snapped, the fire in his eyes now a raging inferno.

A short silence descended over the room. Finally, Rick nodded, looking both uncomfortable and annoyed. "Fine. I'll call Knight and update him on this latest…development."

After Rick left the room, Blake shifted in his chair so that they were face-to-face.

They eyed each other for a long moment. Her heart unwittingly did a flip-flop. The turbulent expression in his eyes reminded her of the way he'd looked when he'd kissed her last night.

She shook her head, wondering how they'd gotten from

point A—passionately kissing last night—to point B—hurling threats at each other today.

She released a regretful breath. "I'm not going to call a press conference," she finally murmured.

"I'm not going to arrest you," he murmured back, a wry flicker in his eyes.

"So what are we going to do about this?"

He rubbed his chin and she found herself wishing it was her own hand stroking that well-defined jaw. Heat speared into her skin, catching her off guard. God, this wasn't the time to be thinking about kissing him again.

"Sam, you can't stay."

His gaze rested on her mouth, and suddenly she knew he wasn't talking about the case, or the danger she faced by sticking around.

Her reaction to his nearness couldn't have been have been more clear if it were pasted on a billboard on Lakeshore Drive. Her nipples poked against the thin lace of her bra, that place between her thighs ached, and her cheeks were so warm she knew they must be flushed. She might have been embarrassed about the obvious arousal he brought out in her, if not for the same sense of awareness radiating from him. His pulse vibrating in his strong neck, his eyes darkening to smoky whiskey. He wanted her, the same way she wanted him.

The air between them hummed, and the tension hissing in the room only heightened her response. She hadn't thought she could feel this way around a man again, but her body, reduced to its most basic, primal state, was practically singing for him to touch her.

Blake saw the arousal glimmering in Sam's big gray eyes and his groin hardened. Dammit. Not now. Not this woman.

"Blake…" The soft word broke through the sexual tension sizzling between them. "I need to be here to see this thing through."

"Don't you care that you'll be putting yourself in danger?" Frustration poured out of his voice, but he wasn't sure if it was due to her determination to place herself in harm's way, or because of the heat pulsing through his veins.

His mouth tingled with the need to kiss her again.

She folded her hands over her lap. "I'm not stupid, Blake. I won't go charging through the city, yelling for the bastard to come and get me. I just want to help."

Alarm trickled through him. "Help how?"

"Looking through mug shots, helping you talk through things as I did today. I can't hide from him anymore."

Her delicate chin lifted with fortitude and a strangled groan escaped from his lips. A part of him wanted to throw her over his shoulder and haul her out the door. Another part wanted to carry her into his bedroom and make love to her until neither of them could move.

She leaned forward, providing him with an eyeful of the delicious cleavage swelling from the neckline of her thin, green sweater. "Let me stay here with you, Blake."

"Here?" he echoed.

His mouth grew so dry it felt like someone had stuffed a dozen cotton balls inside it. She wanted to stay *here?* With *him?* And turn his cozy home into the Garden of Eden, forbidden fruit and all?

She must have seen the disinclination in his eyes, because she frowned. "I'm trying to compromise. I refuse to be carted off to Florida but I'm willing to accept protection, Blake. If I stay with you, you'll keep me safe. You'll protect me."

Something hard and agonizing slammed into him.

"Come on, Blake, let me come along."

"Katie, it's too dangerous."

"You'll protect me."

The sound of Kate's voice in his head stole the breath right out of his lungs. *You'll protect me.* The same words Sam had just said, the same task he'd failed to carry out the last time a woman had asked for his protection.

He'd probably always blame himself for Kate's death. It was a reality he lived with, one he'd accepted, yet he'd learned that the only way to function normally in his life and his job was to keep the memory of Kate buried in the back of his mind. That's why he'd thrown himself headfirst into this case. He'd taken it on in hopes that it would distract him, allow him to keep the pain at bay, something his three months' leave a year ago hadn't accomplished.

And here he was, right back in the same position. He'd hoped that hunting another killer would make him forget the loss of the woman he'd loved. Instead, he was now facing losing a woman he was starting to care about.

And dammit, he did care about Sam. He barely knew her, yet he was feeling things for her he'd never thought he would feel again. Admiration. Respect.

Lust.

Oh, yeah, definitely lust. He wanted her so bad he could taste her on his tongue.

God help him.

"You won't change your mind about this, will you?"

"No," she said, her tone firm.

With a sigh, he rose from his chair and left the dining room. He found Rick pacing the front hallway and murmuring into his cell phone.

"Let me talk to him," Blake said, holding out his hand.

Rick tossed him the phone without a word.

"What's going on there, Corwin?" Knight barked.

"She's going to stay here with me." From the corner of his eye he saw Sam appear in the doorway. She watched him, a whisper of a smile lifting her sensual mouth. "I'll do everything in my power to keep Miss Dawson safe."

"You'll be taking full responsibility should anything happen?"

He struggled to maintain a calm voice. "Yes."

"Fine. She's under your protection."

"Thank you, sir."

He hung up and handed the phone back to Rick, who shot him a quizzical look. "You sure about this, Blake?"

His gaze slid in Sam's direction. "I don't seem to have a choice in the matter."

He wasn't happy with her. Sam could sense it as she watched Blake rub his temples. He did that a lot, almost like he had one continuous headache that simply couldn't be remedied. Was she the source of tonight's headache? Oh, yeah. No question about it. He definitely wasn't pleased that she'd decided to stay in the city.

Rick had just left, which meant that she and Blake were officially alone. Her throat tightened at the thought. Even though she'd convinced him to let her stay, knowing they'd be in such close quarters made her apprehensive. Before the attack she would've capitalized on the coziness of the situation. Now she didn't know what she was going to do. She didn't know why her body had decided to wake up after six months of hibernation, didn't know why Blake was the man who'd spurred the awakening. But what she did know, without a doubt, was that she wanted this man.

She wanted his stubborn mouth kissing hers again. She wanted to tangle her fingers in his messy dark hair and lose herself in his tall, sturdy body. She wanted those serious whiskey-colored eyes to look at her with passion again, wanted to hear that rough voice telling her she was beautiful.

Maybe it was crazy to want so much. Maybe none of those delicious things would come to be. But if she left town there wouldn't even be a chance. Here, she could hope, and dream, and dammit, *want*.

"Knight requests that you lay low," Blake said as they drifted back into the dining room. He moved his hand from his temples to the faint stubble shadowing his jaw. "You'll be able to talk to Elaine on the phone, but you're not leaving this house. Not until the media storm dies down."

"All right."

"The Chicago PD is stationing a car outside the house, and when I meet with the task force at the end of the week, an officer will be here with you."

Again she said, "All right."

"Are you hungry?"

The sudden change of subject caught her by surprise. Her stomach, however, seemed to be waiting for the question, for it instantly growled in response.

She gave a faint smile. "Starved."

"I'll fix us something."

He disappeared into the kitchen, leaving her sitting at the table to contemplate his strange behavior. Once it had been decided that he'd be acting as her own personal bodyguard, his entire demeanor had shifted, becoming stiff, professional. She didn't like it. She'd grown used to the warmth radiating from him, the impression that he actually gave a damn about what happened to her. He still did, of course, but his impersonal manner made her feel as if she were being viewed as an assignment now, and not a woman.

She'd just have to change that, wouldn't she?

Twenty minutes later Blake rejoined her in the dining room. He set two plates on the table, along with two glasses and a bottle of red wine, then bounded into the kitchen again. He returned with a large serving bowl of spaghetti, topped with plain tomato sauce that had probably come out of a can.

"I can't cook anything else," he said with an endearing shrug of one shoulder.

His gruff voice brought a smile to her lips. "It looks great."

Looking as if he didn't quite believe her, Blake piled the pasta onto her plate, then moved to his own chair and served himself. He pulled the cork from the wine bottle and poured each of them a glass, then dug into his food silently.

As she ate, Sam's gaze strayed to the window. The drapes were open, but all she saw was a curtain of white against the windowpane. Fat snowflakes floated in front of the glass, making her smile. God, she loved winter. She'd always looked forward to the first snow of the season, greeting it every year by slipping her knee-length Burberry coat over her shoulders, tucking her hair under a wool hat, and walking through the snow in her favorite pair of high-heeled leather boots.

This year she'd watched that first snowfall from behind a locked window in the farmhouse in Wellstock.

"Let's go for a walk," she blurted.

Blake lifted his head. He focused for a moment on the snow falling outside before letting out a sigh that seemed unrelated to the weather. "I don't think that's possible. If any of my neighbors recognized you…"

Her face fell as he trailed off. He was right, of course. And since he'd already agreed to let her stay here with him, she didn't want to push her luck by parading through the neighborhood and getting recognized again. The last thing she wanted was Blake changing his mind and sending her away.

He must have seen the disappointment in her eyes because he released another breath. "What if we went out into the backyard?" he suggested. "Won't be much of a walk but it's a pretty nice yard."

Abandoning her half-eaten food, she said, "Sounds good."

She didn't have her Burberry coat or her favorite boots, but she made do with the black bomber jacket Blake grabbed for her. The coat hung down to her knees, and the sexy masculine scent imprinted in the material wrapped around her like a warm embrace.

The kitchen door opened out into the backyard and the second they stepped into the chilly night air, a smile filled her face. Blake flicked on a light and a yellow glow bathed the snow-covered patio.

"God, it's so beautiful," she breathed, tilting her head to stare up at the inky sky and the snowflakes dancing down from it. "Isn't it gorgeous?"

"It is."

Heat spilled over her cheeks when she realized he wasn't admiring the display of winter around them, but that his dark gaze was focused on her face.

Her heart skipped, then broke out in a frenzied gallop and vibrated against her ribs. Swallowing, she brushed a few wet flakes off her eyelashes and ascended the short set of steps from the patio to the barren yard.

There wasn't a single piece of furniture out there, not even a birdhouse for the sparrows she'd heard chirping outside the guest room window this morning. But the way the falling snowflakes hit the solitary light illuminating the empty yard created an almost magical ambience. She inhaled deeply, savoring the scent of the clean air and the pine trees lining the perimeter of the yard.

The snow began to gather and pile on the ground under their feet. "Think there'll be a blizzard tonight?" she asked as she stuck her hands in the pockets of her coat.

"I hope not." He paused, then added, "You know, blizzards were the bane of my childhood existence."

"Why is that?"

"My mother always used a blizzard as an excuse to launch into family game night. When I was growing up, a storm was the only thing that would get the entire family in the same room, all five of us trapped indoors. Mom would sit us down in front of the fireplace and pull out those God-awful board games."

"Come on, it couldn't have been that bad," she teased when she heard the exasperation in his tone.

He thought about it for a moment. "You're right. It wasn't as bad as I make it out to be." A smile tugged at his mouth. "Mark, my brother, would force us to play Monopoly, and he'd go around the board buying every property until he ran out of money in the first ten minutes. My sister Jess cheated up a storm, stealing hundreds from the bank when she thought we weren't looking."

"And your parents?"

Blake laughed. "Dad would fall asleep before he reached Go for the first time, and Mom pretended to like the game when really she just liked spending time with us. And me, well, I'd always win, of course."

"Of course." She didn't miss the fondness in his tone when he spoke of his family, and a pang of longing tugged at her belly. She averted her eyes before he could see the sadness in them.

Apparently she didn't break the eye contact fast enough. "Hey, what's wrong?" he murmured.

She sighed. "I'm just envious, that's all. Beau and I never had any family gatherings like that growing up."

"Your file said your parents died when you were sixteen. That should have been plenty of time for family togetherness."

"Not really. My parents were both lawyers. They owned their own firm, and they spent seven days a week in the office. Beau and I had a nanny." She laughed softly. "Her name was Hilda, and she was an absolute nightmare. Her idea of fun was making us help her wash the windows. But she spent time with us at least, which is more than I can say for our parents."

Blake reached out and took her hand. She glanced at it for a moment but said nothing. It seemed like a subconscious move on his part, and she liked the feel of his warm fingers against her palm too much to draw attention to it and risk him taking his hand away.

"That must have been tough," he said.

"It was." She shot him a sideways glance. "But I had my brother. He's five years older, so he thought I was a pain in the ass most of the time, but he was always there for me when I needed him. After our parents died he even put off going to college so he could live at home with me until I finished high school."

"What does he do for a living?"

"He's an artist. A painter. And argue with him all you want, but he'll never consider any of the photographs I've posed for as art. He always hated my career."

"Did you like it, though? Modeling?" He rubbed the inside of her palm with his thumb. She took a sharp intake of breath. Oh, God. His touch felt like heaven against her cold hands. She wanted so badly to lace her fingers through his, but held back, afraid if she did he'd become rigid and professional again.

"I liked it a lot, actually. I started out doing catalogue work, seasonal stuff for department stores, that kind of thing. Then my agent got me a go-see for a swimsuit magazine, and my career took off." She grinned. "I was lucky enough to travel to some incredible places. Gosh, I can't even begin to describe it. I remember this one shoot in Bora Bora, a rock-climbing spread—wearing a bikini, mind you—and it was unbelievable."

He looked surprised. "Wait, that was an actual mountain you were on? In that picture with the yellow bikini?"

Pleasure suffused her entire body. "You saw the spread?"

He actually blushed, which made her heart do a couple of jumping jacks. There was nothing sexier than a man who was man enough to blush.

"I may have come across it," he said grudgingly.

"Admit it," she teased. "You were a fan." Her eyes twinkled. "I could sign an autograph for you, if you'd like."

He let out a laugh and held his palm over his heart. "An autograph from a real-life swimsuit model? I'd be honored."

"Now you're making fun of me," she grumbled. She gave him a wry look. "You probably think what I did was sleazy, huh? Putting myself on display like that."

"Sleazy? No. Sexy? Yes, ma'am."

Her stomach did a happy little flip. "What if I told you I only started modeling to stick it to my parents?"

"Was that the case?"

She nodded. "They were already gone by the time a modeling agent discovered me, but it didn't matter. All my life I wanted them to notice me, and they never did. When I told them I had no interest in going to law school, it got even worse. Beau had already disappointed them by deciding to be an artist, so I guess my decision not to go into law was the final straw. That's when I became completely invisible."

"I can't even fathom how you could be invisible to anyone."

"Well, I was." She shrugged. "And then I started modeling and suddenly everyone noticed me. I loved the attention, loved the sense of importance that came with it, even if I was only important to a few designers and some drooling men." Her voice hardened. "Until the wrong person noticed me."

She stalked past him, nearly slipping on the frost-covered grass. Blake hurried after her and pressed both hands on her shoulders to keep her steady.

"It wasn't your fault, Sam," he said quietly.

Her shoulders drooped. "If I hadn't chosen to put my body on display, he might never have found me."

"Hey, don't think like that. You didn't do a thing to provoke the attack. Neither did Elaine or the others. None of you deserved what that psychopath did to you, none of you asked for it. Bad luck and the misfortune of being in the wrong place at the wrong time, Samantha. That's all it was."

He sounded so earnest, so sure of himself, that tears pricked her eyelids. How did this man know exactly what to say and do to make her feel better? And why, when she should be focusing on putting the man who hurt her behind bars, did she want nothing more than to kiss Blake Corwin again? For six months she'd dreaded the thought of a man touching her. Shied away from it. Now she wanted Blake to touch her. Over and over again.

As if sensing her need, he stepped closer. Lazy flakes of snow floated down between them, tickling Sam's nose and sticking in her hair, but she couldn't make her hands brush the snow away. She couldn't take her eyes off Blake. The scent of him filled her nose—heady, masculine. His gaze flickered with desire and uncertainty, as if he were torn between pulling her close and pushing her way.

God, she didn't want him to push her away. It had been so

long since she'd felt this way, since she'd wanted so badly to draw someone close and never let go.

"Blake…"

Her voice trailed, her lips unable to form the words she really wanted to say. So she reached out slowly and pressed one palm to his chest. His coat was unzipped, and even with her hand touching the thick material of his sweater, sinew and rock-hard muscle filled her palm.

A wave of warmth and desire lapped over her breasts, tickled her thighs and settled promptly in her core. And in its wake, prickling shivers teased every nerve ending and caused her pulse to quicken to a fevered rate.

God, this was crazy, how badly she wanted him. So badly that every part of her grew hot and damp.

Heat and hunger mingled in her blood. When she tilted her head and saw the same heat and hunger reflecting in his eyes, an unbearable combination of raw need and unadulterated lust filled her body.

His ragged breaths seared her cheek, her skin tingled and trembled at his nearness. As his brown eyes darkened to a smoldering hue, time stopped. They stared at each other.

He seemed to read her mind again as he reached out and traced the outline of her jaw with his thumb, then stroked her lower lip with his fingers. He dipped his head, his warm breath tickling her face, his hands stirring something hot and primal inside her.

She parted her lips. Waited for his kiss.

It never came.

Before she could blink, he drew back. Broke the contact and sent disappointment spiraling through her.

"The snow's getting heavier," he said thickly, avoiding her gaze. "We should go back inside."

Chapter 8

The next morning Blake received a phone call from Rick, who offered his trademark brand of good, bad and terrible news.

"The lab came back with a report on the dirt we found on Elaine Woodman's body," Rick said briskly. "It was identified as a slow-release fertilizer."

Hope spurted in Blake's chest, causing him to grip the phone more tightly. "Did you narrow it down to any growers in the area who use that type of fertilizer?"

"Unfortunately, every grower in the damn city uses it. Chasing the trail will only lead to thousands of potential suspects. We need more to go on. But the detectives on the task force are looking into the florist angle as we speak."

"What about the blood and tissue samples collected at the warehouse?"

"A bust. The blood belonged to one person—Elaine. And the skin cells found under her fingernails were contaminated. The tech only managed to get a partial profile. All we know is that our guy is male. We ran the profile through CODIS. No hits." Rick's voice grew somber. "There's more."

"There always is."

"Our pictures were in the paper this morning."

He nearly dropped the phone. "What?"

"The reporter, Reynolds, he did some digging and found some old photos of us at the press conference Knight held after Butcher Betty was captured." Rick hesitated. "Reynolds also mentioned running into you and Samantha in the hospital and announced that she was under your protection."

Blake's jaw tightened. "So if our guy is watching the news or reading the papers, he knows our faces."

"And our names. Yep, that son of a bitch Reynolds went ahead and released those, too."

Just freaking great. "All right," he said with a sigh. "Thanks for letting me know."

"Knight says to keep Samantha out of sight while we look into the florist theory. He doesn't want her gallivanting around in public and attracting unwanted attention."

"Don't worry, she's not going anywhere."

He hung up the phone and headed to the kitchen counter, where he poured himself a cup of black coffee. He thought about what transpired between him and Sam last night, how he'd almost kissed her, and heat surged through him, accompanied by a flicker of agitation. Dammit. He needed to stop this. These growing feelings for Sam would only complicate matters.

His chest constricted as he remembered how beautiful she'd looked standing under the falling snow, her dark hair cascading down her slender shoulders, her eyes glimmering with passion. He either deserved a medal for his restraint, or a kick in the shin for the sheer stupidity of pushing away a woman like Samantha Dawson.

He was leaning toward the shin kick when her sleepy voice filled the kitchen.

"Morning," she murmured, offering a tiny yawn that brought a smile to his lips.

With her thin nightshirt hanging over her knees and her brown hair tousled from sleep, she was the prettiest sight he'd seen in a very long time.

"Good morning," he responded, leaning against the counter with his mug in hand.

"There'd better be enough coffee left for me. I'm still half-asleep."

"Isn't it too early to start making demands?"

"Demands?" She snorted. "A model doesn't demand. She is simply given."

He threw his head back and laughed.

"It's true," she insisted, her eyes twinkling. "The life of a model has its perks."

"Yeah, like what?"

She looked thoughtful as she poured herself some coffee. "You know when you go to a fancy-pants restaurant and the maître d' tells you there aren't any tables? Well, he's totally putting you on. There was always a table for me, you know, being a VIP and all." Her eyes sparkled playfully.

"Of course," he said graciously.

"And then there was traveling first-class all the time. Seriously, never fly unless it's first-class." She stared at him with wide eyes, as if she'd just stumbled upon the Hope Diamond at a garage sale. "Did you know they give you *slippers?*"

"My God. I can't believe I've been missing out on first-class slippers all these years."

She jabbed her finger in the air. "Hey, those slippers were unbelievably comfortable." She sipped her coffee, then broke out in a sexy grin. "Oh, and I met Brad Pitt once."

He faked a jaw drop.

"Yeah, that jaw better be dropping," she teased. "That one-minute meeting was a highlight of my life. You know what he said to me?" She didn't wait for him to hazard a guess. "'Nice to meet you'! How wild is that?"

"Definitely wild," he agreed, unable to keep the amusement out of his tone.

He loved seeing her like this. Lighthearted, happy, chattering on about airplane slippers and some actor she'd met. During their first encounter back at the farmhouse, he'd thought the trauma she'd faced had sucked the life out of her. But he was wrong. *This* was the real Samantha Dawson. The laughter dancing in her stormy gray eyes. The relaxed yet elegant demeanor. The tiny grin curving her full rosy lips.

Dear Lord, he wanted to kiss her. Just pull her into his arms and devour her mouth while he touched every inch of her gorgeous body.

Suppressing the urge, he lifted his mug to his lips and took a long sip. As he watched her to do the same, a thought suddenly came to mind.

"What is it?" she asked, sensing his indecision to speak.

"When this is over…will you go back to modeling?"

The joy drained from her face and he immediately regretted the question. "No," she answered quietly.

"Because of the scar?"

She paused, biting her bottom lip in a sweet way that made his chest squeeze. "It's not the scar," she finally admitted. "The past six months I've told myself the scar is the reason I don't want to pose for a camera again, but I don't think that's it, Blake. I got a second chance when I survived the attack and this time around I want...more."

"And what exactly does that mean?"

"After the Rose Killer is behind bars, I think I'll say goodbye to all the excitement of my old life. I find myself wanting things I never imagined I'd want before. A husband, children, family game nights like the ones you described to me. Hell, maybe I'll even leave the city for good, buy that old farmhouse up in Wellstock."

He arched a brow. "A few days ago you refused to go back— now you actually look excited at the prospect of returning."

Sam shrugged. "It really is a pretty town, still close to the city, but quaint, peaceful. The house is old, but with a little fixing up it'll be good as new. It would actually be a great place to raise kids."

Blake's breath caught in his throat as a vivid image flashed before his eyes. Sam, her belly swollen with a baby. Their baby. A little girl with gray eyes like her mother. Maybe a boy, too. And—laughter and the sound of little feet making tracks on that old faded floor of the farmhouse he and Sam would fix up.

Whoa.

As quick as lightning, he shoved the images out of his head, his heart pounding so hard his ribs ached.

"Blake, what's wrong?"

He gulped and met her look of concern. "What? Nothing's wrong."

"You're pale." She reached up and touched his cheek. "Where were you just now?"

Another gulp. "I was just thinking...about the case."

"It'll be all right. You don't need to worry."

He didn't need to worry? Like hell he didn't. He'd just envisioned a future with this woman, right down to the number of kids they'd have.

He tried to gather his composure and regain control. Damn, getting distracted by thoughts like this was outrageously wrong. It was ludicrous. He should be focused on protecting her, which meant keeping his emotions in check, for Sam's safety if nothing else. Fortunately he was spared from coming up with a response thanks to the ring of his cell phone.

He moved to the end of the counter and glanced at the caller ID. Rick again. "I've got to take this," he said to Sam as he lifted the phone to his ear.

Holding her cup, she drifted to the doorway. "I should get dressed. I should call my brother, too. He's probably going crazy wondering what I'm up to."

Blake nodded absently and pressed the talk button on the cell, seeing Sam leave the kitchen from the corner of his eye. He greeted Rick, listened for a moment.

Then he went pale.

Sam knew calling her brother was a mistake the second the connection was made. Pressing the cordless phone to her ear, she sank on the edge of the bed in the guest room and rolled a pair of thick wool socks onto her bare feet, trying not to groan at her brother's accusatory tone.

"You said it was only going to be one day," Beau grumbled from the other end of the line, not bothering with pleasantries like *Hello* or *How are you*.

She could practically picture that telltale crease of worry on her brother's forehead. "There was a change of plans."

Sarcasm poured freely from his voice. "Yeah, everyone knows you're alive. Tell those FBI agents they did a stand-up job."

"It was my fault. I'm the one who wanted to visit Elaine again."

"I never took you for a fool, Sammy. What if this maniac comes after you again?"

"It'll be okay," she said, amazed by the steadiness of her voice. "I promise."

"Shouldn't I be the one who says that?"

"Yeah, but I know you don't believe it."

"Do you?"

Her peripheral vision caught a flash of movement. Turning her head, she found Blake leaning against the doorframe. It only took one glance in his direction to bring a rush of reassurance through her body.

"Yeah, I believe it'll be okay. The FBI will protect me."

"They'd better. Tell that agent you're staying with that if one hair on your head is harmed, I will come after him."

She smothered back a grin. "I'll pass the message along."

She hung up the phone and fixed her gaze on Blake. He looked dead serious, the graveness of his eyes causing a small wave of alarm to wash over her.

"Is everything okay?" she asked.

He hesitated for a moment. "Something's happened."

"What is it?"

"Someone paid a visit to your house this morning."

Her heart stopped. "The farmhouse in Wellstock? I thought that location was supposed to be secure!"

"Not the farmhouse, Sam. I'm talking about the house you lived in before your, uh, death."

"But it was sold two months ago. Someone broke in?" Her anxiety escalated faster than a fighter jet in takeoff. "Were the new owners hurt?"

He shook his head slowly.

The alarm in her chest deepened to full-blown panic, constricting her airways. "Tell me what happened, Blake," she squeaked out.

He spoke in a flat tone. "The new owners are vacationing in the Caribbean and aren't due back for a couple more weeks. The neighbor who'd been collecting their mail called the police reporting that the front yard is covered with roses. Hundreds of them."

Her body shook so hard it was almost impossible to get out the next words. "He was there…at my old house?"

A grim look darkened Blake's eyes. "It seems the Rose Killer has decided to deliver a message."

Blake's gaze swept over the endless carpet of roses. The lush red petals covered the snowy lawn like an enormous pool of blood, the crimson display contrasting sharply with the clean white snow gracing the neighboring yards.

The bastard had been here. He'd approached Samantha's old home—the one he'd once broken into, the one where he'd attacked her—and sprinkled these flowers on the lawn in broad daylight. The sheer nerve of the madman slammed into Blake like a sledgehammer to the chest. And yet the reason for this sick demonstration hadn't become clear yet. Was the son of a bitch taunting them? Did he think Sam still owned the house? Or perhaps this wasn't the handiwork of the Rose Killer at all. Perhaps someone familiar with the case had decided to indulge in a twisted prank.

Although the latter would be a hell of a lot less terrifying, Blake's gut was screaming that this wasn't the work of a prankster.

Rick came up beside him. "You should've stayed with Sam."

"Melanie is with her." He exhaled slowly. "I had to see this for myself."

"You think it's him?"

"Don't you?"

"Oh, yeah. It's him," Rick said grimly. "My instincts are telling me he was here."

"Mine, too."

"The uniforms just finished questioning every resident on the street," Rick added. "Nobody saw a goddamn thing."

Blake wasn't surprised. Most of the people he'd spoken to in the past hour had admitted to being indoors all morning. A few ten-year-olds had been tossing snowballs at each other near the house earlier, but they insisted the roses hadn't been in the yard when they were out there. The boys had headed indoors around eleven. And just past noon, the elderly neighbor across the street had phoned the police, which meant the Rose Killer had been in the vicinity between eleven and twelve.

One hour. That's all it had taken for him to dump several hundred roses on his former victim's lawn. Unfortunately, the snowplows had come through the neighborhood sometime within that same hour, eliminating the hope of finding any usable tire tracks. And the front path leading to the house was devoid of footprints; from the shapeless streaks, they'd deduced that the Rose Killer had kicked the snow as he'd walked to avoid leaving a distinctive mark.

"He knows she's alive," Blake muttered. "He wants us to know that he knows it."

"I think there's more to it than that…"

He saw the wheels turning in his partner's head and waited for Rick to continue.

"I think he was hoping to draw her out into the open. Maybe he doesn't know the house was sold, or maybe he was stupid enough to think we'd bring her along to check out the scene." Rick rubbed his forehead. "I'm just getting a feeling this is more than sending us a message. I think he hoped to achieve something."

"God, I hope not." He paused. "Just in case, we should tell the officers to canvas the neighborhood and check for any suspicious persons loitering around."

"And look out for a tail when you're driving home," Rick added. "He knows our faces. Maybe he's hoping one of us will lead him to Sam."

The idea that the Rose Killer had done this in the hopes of learning Sam's whereabouts was more frightening than the time Blake had gotten lost in the woods during a family vacation when he was seven years old. He'd felt helpless then, powerless, unable to protect himself from the strange noises and forbidding shadows surrounding him in that forest. Fortunately, his father had found him before night had settled in, and over the years Blake had learned to protect himself from the dangerous killers he hunted for a living.

And now he had to protect Sam from another one of those dangerous killers.

His entire body tensed, his jaw so tight his teeth started to hurt. Anger filled his veins at the sight of the red petals strewn across the snow. If that bastard planned on getting his sadistic hands on Sam again, he had another thing coming.

"Blake looked angry," Sam said, her gaze straying to the doorway for the hundredth time that hour.

She kept expecting Blake to walk through the front door, stroll into the living room and tell her it was a false alarm. Nope, the Rose Killer hadn't tossed roses all over her old yard, just the local gardener hoping to bring some color to the neighborhood.

You are definitely losing it.

She tried not to sigh. God, maybe she was losing it. *Of course* the roses had been delivered by the madman who'd attacked her. Who else would be that sick and twisted?

Next to her, Special Agent Melanie Barnes, a tiny waif of a woman with a blond pixie cut, offered a reassuring smile. She wrapped her fingers around the cup of coffee sitting on the kitchen table in front of her. "I'm sure he's fine. He's not always this intense, you know. He's under a lot of pressure, that's all."

"Rick said the same thing to me a few days ago," Sam admitted. "But to be honest, I can't see Blake not being this intense. I think intensity is part of his genetic makeup."

A faint smile crossed Mel's face. "You're probably right. But trust me, I've seen Blake let loose a time or two. He was engaged to a profiler out in Quantico, who used to drag him out of the house whenever he got too moody."

"She died, didn't she—the woman he was involved with?"

Mel looked surprised. "He told you?"

"Not a lot. I only know she died."

"Did he tell you how?"

Sam swallowed. "No."

"Three shots to the back." Mel's voice was curt, but the pain in it was unmistakable. "By a serial killer Blake had been tracking."

Sam wrinkled her forehead. "I thought you said she was a profiler. Do profilers usually go into the field?"

The blond agent shook her head.

"Then why did—"

She was interrupted by the sound of the front door creaking open.

Mel was on her feet just as Blake strode into the kitchen. "Rick's waiting for you outside," Blake told his colleague.

Mel shot him a questioning glance but he gave a slight shake of the head. "Rick will fill you in."

With a nod of her own, Mel turned to Sam. "It was a pleasure meeting you."

She offered a genuine smile. She really had enjoyed spending the last couple of hours with Melanie. It had been so long since she'd had some female company. "Could you let Elaine know I'll call her tonight?"

Mel returned the smile. "She'll appreciate that, Samantha."

After the blonde left, Blake headed for the counter and poured himself a cup of coffee. He didn't say a word as he sipped the hot liquid. She noticed that his shoulders looked stiff under the black sweater stretching across them, his strong jaw taut with displeasure.

"Well?" she asked. "Do you think it was him?"

There was a moment of silence. Blake finally nodded. "Nobody saw a damn thing, but yes, I think it was him."

A sigh slipped out of her chest before she could stop it. She couldn't seem to stop her next words, either. "Don't look so upset."

"You expect me not to be upset?" he returned, his voice laced with steel. "The bastard was at your house, Sam."

"If anything, that's a good thing."

He swiveled his head to shoot her a look swimming with disbelief. "Are you serious? Don't you realize what this means? He knows you're alive. He wants you to know he can come after you again."

"And if he does, you'll be waiting for him."

"I can't believe you're saying this, Sam. You should be worrying about your safety."

She gave a humorless laugh. "I *am* worried about my

safety. As long as this maniac is out on the streets I'll *always* worry about my safety. I'm simply pointing out the positive."

"I'm afraid I don't agree. There's nothing positive about this."

"He must be furious that I'm alive, Blake. So furious that he made the mistake of showing up at my old house in broad daylight. Yes, nobody saw him, but the next time he makes the same mistake he might not be so lucky."

"And what if next time he doesn't make a mistake? What if next time he finishes what he started the night he attacked you?"

His voice, thick with worry, sent a wave of emotion surging through her. He cared about her. She'd never doubted it, but the urgency in his tone told her that Blake Corwin's feelings for her ran much deeper than he'd ever admit.

She thought about the kiss they'd almost shared last night, the one they *had* shared the night before that, and something warm and tender rolled inside her like a balmy summer breeze.

"As long as I'm with you, I'll be fine," she said quietly.

He gave her a sideways glance. "You sound sure of that."

"I am. I have faith that you'll keep me safe, Blake."

The silence that followed was broken by the whistling of wind against the kitchen window. She shifted her gaze and saw fat flakes in front of the glass, falling harder, thicker, as each second ticked by.

"Looks like the blizzard that never came last night decided to make an appearance," she remarked, hoping the change of subject would ease the tension hanging over the room.

Blake gestured to the doorway. "Let's sit in the living room. You'll have a better view of the blizzard from there." His mouth quirked. "I know how much you love watching the snow fall."

Smiling, she followed him into the cozy living room, touched that he was trying to make her feel better about being cooped up indoors by offering to sit by the window and watch the storm with her.

He sank down on the leather couch and sipped his coffee again. His hair fell onto his forehead but he didn't seem to notice or care enough to brush it away, and her fingers tingled with the urge to slide through all that thick dark hair.

She hesitated in the doorway. "I wanted to talk to you about last night," she found herself blurting.

His shoulders instantly stiffened, his face became unreadable.

Dammit. Why was he fighting this? She knew he felt the same hum of awareness she did. Sooner or later he'd have to deal with it, accept that there was...*something*...between them. And since a blizzard was about to rage outside this house, she wasn't going to pass up the opportunity to bring the attraction between them out in the open.

"Why are you doing this?" she asked in a soft voice.

"I'm not doing anything, Sam."

"That's exactly the point." She blew out a frustrated breath. "You were going to kiss me last night."

He fixed that familiar steady gaze on her. "It would have been a mistake."

She sagged against the doorframe, fighting the urge to yell at him. Though there was a good five feet between them, she could feel the heat emanating from his body. The spicy, male scent of him teased her senses and made her want to close the distance. But she knew he'd only shut down if she pushed him too far.

Taking a deep breath, she played with the hem of her sweater, gathered up bits and pieces of the courage she'd once possessed but lost after the attack. "Blake...I'm attracted to you."

He blinked in surprise. Even from where she stood she could see his pulse thudding in his throat.

"You want me to take you to bed, is that it?" His voice was low with both challenge and hesitation.

She swallowed. "Yes."

Chapter 9

Her answer surprised even her, but the second she said it Sam knew she meant it. She wanted her life back, and in order to do that she needed to stop letting fear rule her. She didn't know why Blake had gotten under her skin like this, but he had, and either she could hide from her desire or she could face it head-on.

She glimpsed the brief flash of lust in Blake's eyes, but to her disappointment his expression quickly sobered. "It doesn't bother you that you don't know a thing about the man you want to go to bed with?" he said coolly.

"I know I trust you. I know you'll do anything you can to protect me."

He gave a sarcastic laugh. "The last woman I promised to protect wound up dead, Samantha."

She swallowed. Startling as his admission was, at least they were getting somewhere here. "What was her name?"

His features twisted with pain. "Kate." He cleared his throat. "Her name was Kate."

"Tell me what happened to her." She knew from the bare details Mel provided that Kate had been shot, but she found herself needing to hear it from Blake. Needing to understand the pain that had driven him to decide he didn't "do" relationships anymore.

His handsome face donned a faraway expression. "That's another story for another day."

A frown tugged her mouth down. "Fine. But what about today, what about right now? What about this—whatever *this* is between us? You can't run away from it, Blake."

He rubbed his temples, a gesture she now associated with frustration. "What I don't get is why *you're* not running away, Sam. Correct me if I'm wrong, but I'd be the first man you were with since the attack."

"Yes."

"So why push it? Why do you want me?" He let out a heavy breath. "Is this one of those extreme circumstance syndromes? I've seen it happen before, you know. People caught up in dangerous, stressful situations, needing to get physical in order to feel alive."

She stared at him, incredulous. How wonderful. Here she was practically propositioning this man, and he was accusing her of having a *syndrome.*

"Trust me," she said in a dry voice. "It's not that. Remind me to tell you about the time I was shooting a bikini layout in the dead of winter in Alaska. That was pretty stressful and I don't recall jumping the photographer to make myself feel alive."

Amusement flickered in his eyes, but it was short-lived. "Why do you want me, Sam?"

"Because…" Her voice drifted.

A wave of restlessness washed over her, driving her toward the window. Outside the blizzard grew stronger, piling the street with mounds of blinding-white snow. The wind rattled the house, howling like the crack of a whip against the thick window of Blake's living room.

It was the kind of storm that brought lovers together, sent them rushing to a big warm bed to lose themselves in each other's arms. Not her and Blake, though. No, they had to dig up old wounds and revisit raw memories.

She turned to face him, leaning against the cool glass, shutting out the powerful display of winter behind her. "I'm going to tell you exactly why I want you, Blake. I'm going to pour my heart out to you. And then, *then* you can decide if you want to go forward." She faltered. "Or if you still want to push me away."

She moved back to the center of the room, this time sitting at the edge of the large glass coffee table in front of the couch. She heard his intake of breath at her nearness but he said nothing. Just looked at her with unreadable eyes.

"I know you saw the crime-scene photos from my house," she began, trying to ignore the fingers of bitterness clawing up her throat. "But those were just pictures, words compiled to form a tidy little report for your profilers to analyze."

As if he sensed where she was going, he said, "Sam, you don't have to—"

"He tied me up, facedown, to my own bed. He tore off my dress and I lay there naked, convinced he would not only rape me, but slit my throat." She paused. "You never found the knife, did you? Not in any of your pictures because he took it with him. But I saw it, Blake."

She stopped again, willing every morsel of strength she possessed to keep the pain at bay, far enough away so that she didn't break down.

"It was steel, big and sharp and it shone in the little bit of light coming through the window. He held it to my throat, dragged it over my body instead of using his fingers. I told myself that if I ever survived I would never let another man touch me. But I let you."

"Sam, please—"

"Then he dug the blade into my skin. I was crying, the pain was so excruciating. I passed out from it, but woke up just as he made the first cut in my left wrist."

"Goddammit, Samantha—"

"He sliced my other one. I couldn't see him, but I could feel him standing there and watching me. Watching me bleed." She never took her eyes off Blake's. "I told myself that if I survived I'd never let another man look at me that way. I'd never be vulnerable again, never give anyone the opportunity to *make* me vulnerable. But you did, Blake."

She rose slowly, reaching for the hem of her sweater before pulling it over her head. She wore a pink lace bra underneath and Blake's dark eyes darted unmistakably to her chest and rested on her covered breasts.

"I want you because you make me feel alive. Because I trust myself to be vulnerable when I'm with you. And because I trust that you can look at this and not be disgusted."

She fought for air, closing her mouth before the sob in her throat could slip out. And then she turned around and gave him a candid eyeful of the eight-inch scar on her back.

Sam could feel his gaze burning into her skin and was grateful that she couldn't see his expression. The scar had healed nicely. No longer the angry red slashes that formed together to create a rose. Just faded pink lines that would one day become white, or disappear entirely if she chose to undergo the surgery the doctors had suggested. None of that mattered, though.

To her it would always be a sickening reminder that a madman had branded her. An ugly symbol of the night that had changed her life.

"It's not pretty, is it?" she whispered.

She heard his pants rustle as he stood up. Her first thought was that he would walk away in horror, and that caused a chill to sweep up her body and tighten like a vise around her heart.

"It's beautiful."

Those two soft words broke through her fears. "What?"

She felt him come up behind her, and then his big warm hands were touching her exposed skin. He traced each line of raised tissue with his fingers, replacing the chill with a pulsing heat that spread over all he touched. His caress was gentle, erotic, and in response her knees trembled, buckled beneath her.

Strong hands gripped her waist, keeping her steady. She nearly keeled over again when something hot pressed against her shoulder. His mouth. A cross between a moan and a whimper slid out of her throat. Her skin quivered under his lips. He kissed the sensitive spot between her shoulder blades, then kneeled down and dragged his mouth lower. Ran his tongue languidly over the rose carved into her.

"You've got a war wound, Samantha," he said huskily, slowing moving up her body and wrapping his arms around her from behind. He pressed his lips to one side of her neck. "You could have given up and died that night, but you didn't. You fought like hell to stay alive, didn't you?"

Her eyelids fell closed as he took her earlobe in his mouth and suckled it. "Yes."

"That's what that rose represents to me," he said hoarsely. "It's a symbol of your strength, Sam."

He didn't let her answer, simply whirled her around and crushed her in his embrace. Their mouths found each other with little difficulty, their tongues danced together as if they'd done this hundreds of times before.

He rested his hands on her bare back, sending heat pulsating down to her most intimate place. Her knees buckled again and this time he cupped her bottom and lifted her up against him, never tearing his mouth from hers.

Somehow they found their way upstairs to Blake's bedroom, though everything became a blur to her. His lips were too intoxicating, his hands too skilled. Her entire body was on fire, hot with pleasure and heavy with need. She didn't object when Blake gently placed her on the bed.

He reached for the button of her slacks, then paused and met her gaze. "Do you want to stop?" he murmured.

"Do you?"

"I don't think I could, even if I wanted to."

It wasn't the answer she'd wanted, an answer she could even be satisfied with, but it was enough for now.

A shiver sprung up her spine as he pulled down her slacks and exposed the pink cotton panties underneath. She suddenly wished she'd worn sexier lingerie. She wanted to feel beautiful, wanted to *look* beautiful for Blake, but her insecurities diminished when his dark eyes widened at the sight of her barely clad body.

"You're gorgeous," he muttered, running a finger over her lower thigh.

He removed his shirt, revealing a wall of solid, tanned muscle, a chest so spectacular her breath jammed in her throat. She found herself reaching out to touch him, skimmed the light feathering of dark hair that tunneled down and disappeared into the waistband of his pants. She stroked him for a moment, then awkwardly moved her hand, suddenly uncertain.

"It's okay to touch me." He chuckled quietly.

"I…" She bit her lip as trepidation bubbled inside her. "I'm scared, Blake."

The way his features softened with empathy frustrated her. Dammit. Why was this happening? She'd been so sure just moments before, so certain she wanted to do this. Now as she lay in front of him, exposed and vulnerable, her fears rushed back and the only thing she could think of was the night she'd discovered a killer in her bedroom.

Her brain registered that this was Blake in front of her, but her eyes twisted and contorted his image until all she saw was gleaming red eyes and a face veiled by shadows. She slammed her eyelids shut, clamped her mouth so she wouldn't cry out. Panic seized her body. She shuddered violently, and then… then Blake's hand was stroking her cheek.

"I'm not him, Sam." His gentle voice prompted her to open her eyes. "I won't hurt you."

"I know." She *did* know, and yet her muscles refused to relax.

"Do you trust me?" he asked, his gaze steadily meeting hers.

"Yes," she whispered.

"Then we'll take it slow, all right?"

She nodded wordlessly. Watched as he moved closer and stretched his long lean body next to her on the bed. He kept his pants on, but his bare chest still dominated the dimly lit room, making him appear lethal and appealing all at once. His muscles bunched and flexed at each movement, oozing with strength. And his abdomen was rippled, a six-pack so chiseled pioneer women could have washed their clothes on it. He was so unbelievably sexy, so *male*.

When he touched her again she didn't flinch or shudder, just held her breath and let him caress her. His hand moved lower, grazing her neck, her collarbone, gliding over the cleavage jutting from her bra.

She shivered.

He pulled his hand away. "Too much?"

"Not enough," she murmured.

She laced her fingers through his, brought his hand back to her chest and pressed it to one swollen breast. Her panic diminished as he slid a finger under the lacy cup and brushed it over her nipple, sending an exquisite shiver skipping across her body.

He unhooked the front clasp of her bra and her breasts spilled out. As the cool air met her skin, she shivered again, but Blake warmed her right up by lowering his mouth to kiss one pebbled nipple. She gasped as his lips brushed over the tight bud, as his tongue darted out to lick and explore.

Closing her eyes, Sam tried to focus on the delicious sensations coursing through her. Tried to lose herself in the feel of Blake's mouth on her breasts and the teasing abrasions of his five o'clock shadow against her sensitive flesh.

And then his hand slid down her belly toward the juncture of her thighs, and she froze again.

Blake removed his hand. "Maybe we'd better stop."

Disappointment flooded her. "No, I don't want to stop. I just need..." Her voice drifted as she realized that she couldn't even figure out what she needed, let alone vocalize it.

"You need to be in charge," he said in a gentle voice.

"What?"

Without answering, Blake moved over so that he was lying on his back. He propped his arms behind his head. "I could easily have my way with you right now. I could take what I want from you, kiss you, touch you, drive myself inside you. But I won't."

Desire and distress mingled in her blood. The former, because the sensual image he'd just provided sent a spiral of heat to her core. And the latter, because he wasn't going to follow through on it.

"Why not?"

He looked amused at the irritation in her voice. "Because I don't want to take anything from you. I only want to give it. So the way I see it, if this is going to happen, you need to set the pace. Take what you want, Sam. Nothing will frighten you if you're the one making it happen."

A lump formed at the back of her throat. God, who was this man? How did he know exactly what she needed?

"And if I can't go through with it?"

"Then at least you got one step closer."

The rough quality to his voice made her pulse race. She locked her gaze to his. "Okay."

Fingers trembling, she ran her palm over his chiseled pectorals, slowly exploring the feel of his chest. Smooth. Hard. Perfect.

She bent her head to kiss his flat nipple, her own nipples tightening as she felt it harden against her mouth. Then, feeling bold, she licked his skin, reveling in the spicy, masculine taste of him.

He flinched, but kept his hands at his sides. A muscle twitched in his jaw. He didn't try to touch her, or kiss her, or push her to quicken the leisurely pace she'd set, and his restraint only heightened her desire.

She quickly unbuckled his belt. Her fingers shook again as she inched his pants down his muscular thighs, over his defined calves, his hard ankles. He wore blue boxers that hugged his thighs. Sam gulped at the sight of the bulge straining against the cotton material.

Meeting her wide eyes, Blake gave a raspy chuckle. "You've been doing that to me since the day I met you."

Pleasure fluttered through her like a lazy butterfly, followed by an unfamiliar emotion that swept over her body and left shivery tingles in its wake. She was surprised to feel the growing dampness between her legs, and the need to have this man inside her was so strong that her thighs started to shake.

As ripples of impatience suddenly cascaded down to her core, she tugged at the waistband of his boxers. She peeled the fabric off him, then moaned when he sprang free. He was hot and hard and when she touched his tip with her index finger she felt the bead of moisture there.

"Blake?"

"Yes?" He looked at her with such tenderness she almost burst into tears.

"I…" *I need you.* "Don't have protection."

"I do." He leaned over and reached for the end table next to the bed. He rummaged around in the top drawer, pulled out a foil packet and handed it to her.

She glanced down at the condom in her hand and found herself smiling. "Do FBI agents always keep these next to the bed?"

"When a model is staying at their house, yeah."

The crooked grin on his face made her heart skip a beat. She looked at the condom again, then at Blake, and finally tore open the corner of the foil.

She rolled the latex over his arousal. Biting the inside of her cheek, she slid her panties down her legs, moved over him, and straddled his naked lower body with her thighs.

Blake lifted his hands to her hips and searched her face. "Are you sure?"

Was she sure? That terrified little part of her brain told her to say no. Ordered her to run out of the room and hide from the uncontrollable desire he elicited in her.

But her body, and her heart, wouldn't let her. She was so ready, and all she wanted right now was to feel this man inside her. Deep, deep inside her.

She drew in an uneven breath. "I'm sure."

Without allowing herself a moment to change her mind, she slid down and captured him in her softness. Oh, God. The delicious stretching of her body deepened the ache, and the low groan from Blake told her he enjoyed it as much as she did.

"Take your time," he whispered.

She looked down at his rugged features—his brown eyes, firm lips and handsome jaw—and knew that taking her time was not going to be an option. She wanted him. Now.

His hands cupped her bottom as she began to ride him. It was difficult, especially when her knees wouldn't stop shaking and her inner muscles throbbed at each slow thrust. It had been a long time since she'd been with a man, and yet something about this, about Blake, was so different from any past experience. It all felt new, tender, *right*.

Her eyelids fluttered closed, but she quickly blinked them open. Making love to Blake was so achingly wonderful that she didn't want to miss a second of it.

She fell against his chest, buried her head in the hollow of his neck and inhaled the heady scent of him. He smelled so good, felt so good, and her arousal heightened to a level that made it impossible to move.

She heard him chuckle again, and before she could blink, he rolled her over and covered her body with his. They were mouth to mouth, chest to chest, naked skin clinging and sliding, hearts thudding against each other.

"Better?" he rasped.

She nodded. With eyes wide open, she watched him move slowly inside her. Suddenly the pace was all wrong. As beads of sweat dotted her forehead, she clung to him, scraped her fingernails against the strong sinew of his back, grabbed his taut buttocks to pull him in as deep as he could go. *Oh, yes.* She was suddenly frantic, wanting more and more of him, and she lifted her hips off the mattress so she could feel him, all of him.

He thrust into her. Again. And again. Her need rose, climbed, soared, until her eyes finally fluttered and light flashed before her closed lids. She cried out as her climax swirled through her like a wildfire, hot smoldering flames licking every inch of her damp skin. Shards of pleasure exploded inside her, and when she heard Blake's guttural groan, when she felt him shudder with release, another wave of sheer unadulterated bliss rocked into her.

"Samantha," he gasped out, then crushed his mouth against hers and kissed the breath out of her lungs.

She kissed him back, arched her breasts against his big, warm chest and hungrily flicked her tongue against his.

She didn't know how long they lay there, kissing, panting, but she didn't care. For the first time in six months, she felt whole again, and for the moment, that's all that mattered.

She was in that house. Screwing that man. Rubbing her infidelity in his face.

He gripped the steering wheel. Dug his nails into it and imagined that it was something else he was squeezing. Namely her neck.

He'd known the roses would lead him to her. The house in which they'd shared their first encounter was in the hands of new owners but he'd decided it was the perfect setting to make his move and find out if the reporters were right about her survival. He knew showering the lawn with flowers would catch the attention of the police, as well as his prey. She'd always loved his roses, loved them so much she'd had one tattooed below her right breast, where only the man in her bed could see it.

There was a man in her bed now. The Fed whose picture had been in the paper. The reporter claimed he'd seen the cop at the hospital with the woman, and all he'd had to do was wait for the man to lead him to his quarry. Following him had been difficult; he'd almost lost him a few times in order not to be made. But he'd been trained by the best— the United States Army. General Madsen would've been proud, had he been alive. But his old mentor was gone now, died for his country. A country that hadn't even given a damn about him.

He was glad Madsen was in the grave. The general would've been horrified to know what he'd been through. The general would've spit in the faces of those incompetent asshole cops who hadn't thought his best soldier was god-damn "stable" enough to be one of them.

Useless cops. What did they know about honor or courage or fighting for your country? Apparently, all they did was sleep around on the job.

Acid burned his throat, made his eyes water and his veins bubble with poison. The wind rocking the car only infuriated him more. He should be inside that pathetically cheerful-looking brick house, lying in that bed with her. Not sitting outside in the middle of a raging blizzard and longing to have his hands on her throat.

A faint beam of light caught his eyes. Headlights. A police car approached the house, more than likely arriving to guard the filth inside.

He moved the gearshift to Drive and steered down the snowy street. His mouth twisted in a smile. She thought she was safe, that he couldn't touch her as long as she had her big bad cop lover to protect her.

She'd always been a very stupid woman.

He turned at the end of the road and headed toward his sanctuary. She'd be joining him here, very soon. Now that he knew where she was, he could bide his time. Wait for an opening, an opportunity to make his move.

And then he would exact his final punishment.

This time he wouldn't fail.

Chapter 10

By the time five-thirty in the morning rolled around, Blake officially gave up on the notion of sleep. He'd been lying awake for hours, debating whether to kick himself or simply bask in the afterglow of the best sex he'd ever had, and the constant battle in his brain made drifting off into slumber impossible.

He glanced down at Sam's sleeping face and held her warm naked body close to him, knowing it was probably time to throw the FBI-conduct handbook out the window.

He'd been an agent since he was twenty-two years old and in the ten years he'd worked for the Bureau he'd never slept with a witness. And then Samantha Dawson came into his life, and suddenly all he could think about was her silky hair and smoky-gray eyes and that centerfold body that felt too damn good pressed against his.

His chest ached at the memory of the vulnerability he'd seen in Sam's eyes before she'd turned to show him her scar.

He hadn't lied to her; the rose on her back didn't disgust him, didn't make him want to run for the hills. All it did was deepen his desire for her, and as he stared up at the ceiling now, he realized why he felt so troubled.

This wasn't just about lust. Hell, it never had been. Yes, he was attracted to her. Yes, she brought him to a level of arousal he'd never known before. But it was more than that.

Her strength amazed him. Her determination impressed the hell out of him. And her vulnerability brought him to his knees.

He wanted to take care of her. Not because she was a witness or a victim or someone he was paid to protect. He wanted to take care of her the way a man took care of the woman he shared his bed with. Shared his *life* with.

He hadn't felt this way since Kate. And yet it was different. With Kate, it had taken months for them to fall into bed with each other. Months for them to reach that level of sated comfort he now felt lying next to Sam.

"Blake?"

She stirred in his arms. With her cheeks flushed and hair tousled from sleep, she looked tired and satisfied and so beautiful he fought the urge to roll her over and make love to her again.

They'd already spent most of yesterday afternoon in bed, talking and making love for hours, getting out from under the covers only to grab a quick bite before dashing right back into bed. It almost felt wrong, having time to play and unwind while he was in the middle of a case, but Knight had made it clear he didn't want Samantha going out in public, which meant Blake had no choice but to stay by her side. Not that he minded.

"It's early. Go back to sleep," he said gruffly, tangling his fingers in her hair.

"Not until you tell me why you're lying here with a frown on your face." She yawned, then propped up on her elbow.

The sight of her bare breasts distracted him and he couldn't help but reach out and drag his thumb over one rosy nipple.

"Oh, no, you don't," she said, swatting his hand away. "Answer the question."

He smiled in the darkness. "What question?"

"The frown, Blake."

Sensing that she wouldn't let it go, his face grew serious. "I'm just thinking."

"About what?"

"You. This case."

"Will you get in trouble for sleeping with me?"

He laughed at the little girl voice she used. "Not unless I call up my supervisor and give him a play-by-play of yesterday's events." His laugh caught in his throat. "I need this case to be over, Sam."

A shadow crossed her face, and she sat up. She wrapped the blanket over her shoulders and moved into a cross-legged position, her bare knees poking out of the covers.

"It's really taking a toll on you, chasing this guy."

"It hasn't been that bad," he lied.

She gave a soft laugh. "Yeah? So explain the constant headaches. Or that knot between your shoulders that years of massage therapy probably couldn't get out."

"As I said, I want it to be over."

"God, so do I." She sighed. "I want him captured, Blake."

Before he could reply, she tossed the blanket aside and got out of bed. Across the room, a part in the curtains allowed for a sliver of dawn light to stream inside and he couldn't help but admire her smooth, slender body. She looked every inch the model—high, full breasts; hand-span waist; curvy bottom and never-ending legs. His body tightened at the gorgeous sight.

She headed for the foot of the bed, grabbed the shirt he'd been wearing last night and slipped it over her head. His breath hitched. Damn, there was nothing sexier than a woman in a man's shirt.

No, there was nothing sexier than *this* woman in *his* shirt.

"I'll put on a pot of coffee," she said, then disappeared into the hallway.

Blake stayed in bed and closed his eyes, wondering if he should try to force sleep. If he slept, he wouldn't have to think about how he'd just made love to the woman he was supposed to be protecting. Wouldn't need to combat the desire that pulsed through him at the knowledge that Sam was in his kitchen, naked under his shirt.

Unfortunately, he was wide-awake and unable to get the wicked image of Sam out of his mind.

He slid out of bed, put on his boxers and headed downstairs, where he found her leaning against the marble kitchen counter as she waited for the coffee machine to do its thing.

Her gaze immediately went to his bare chest and the small smile she shot him hit him in the gut and made his groin stiffen. He could see why so many men had bought that swimsuit edition. He would've bought ten years of issues just to see that smile.

He crossed the distance between them and pulled her close. Her arms tightened around him. Pressing her lips to his throat, she planted a soft kiss on his skin then buried her face in the crook of his neck. "God, that smells good," she murmured.

"Thank you?"

"I was referring to the coffee."

He offered a rogue grin. "*Sure* you were."

She ran a hand across the nape of his neck and the little hairs there tingled from the warmth of her touch. "You know, you should smile more often. You look nice when you smile."

"I smile," he said defensively.

"Yeah, sure." She snorted. "Face it, most of the time you either look like you've got a migraine, like you're training to climb Everest, or like you're playing golf."

He lifted a brow. "So you see me as a mountain-climbing golfer?" He paused. "Why golf, by the way?"

"Because golfers always look so ridiculously grim. They act like the world will crumble beneath their feet if they don't tap a little white ball into a hole. Frankly, I don't get it. And I'm serious, Blake, you need to lighten up sometimes. You're way too intense."

He shrugged. "Been that way all my life. I take after my father, I guess. He's always been serious. Now my mom, on the other hand—she doesn't know the meaning of serious. And don't get me started on my sister. She's the most cheerful person I've ever met. It's enough to induce a migraine or make me want to climb Everest."

With a laugh, she wiggled out of the embrace. "You make a good point. Perpetually cheerful people *can* be hard to swallow. But I still think you could stand to relax once in a while." She drifted over to the counter and poured the steaming coffee into two tall mugs. "So what should we do today? I haven't had a snow day since grade school."

"What's a snow day?" he returned with a sigh. "My parents never let us stay home the day after a blizzard."

"What if the school was closed?"

"Then Mom would give us impromptu lessons in the living room."

Sam giggled. "Poor thing."

She handed him a mug. A few sips later, the caffeine kicked into gear, pulsed through his blood and made him forget that he'd spent the entire night awake, tossing and turning.

Sam crossed the room and peeked out the window next to the back door. "God, there's so much snow! I can't wait to go out there."

"Sure you wouldn't prefer spending the day in bed?"

She shot him an endearing smile and wagged her finger. "We did that yesterday. Today you get to experience the splendor of a snow day."

He wanted to tell her he'd much rather experience the splendor of *her,* but the light dancing in her gray eyes made him bite his tongue. He thought back to the day he'd first met her, the haunting pain and unmistakable torment he'd seen in those eyes, and he experienced a surge of pleasure knowing he'd been the one to erase it.

It probably wasn't a good idea, going outside now that they knew the Rose Killer suspected she was alive, but the yard was fenced in, and he'd be with her, and...

Oh man, something about this woman made him feel helpless and vulnerable and weak in the knees. All it took was one smile from her, one sexy look, and he was ready to give her anything she wanted.

Even a day of playing in the snow.

"I *cannot* believe you've never made a snow angel before."

Sam stared at Blake with utter disbelief. Was it actually possible that Blake, the man who admitted to family Monopoly nights, had failed to indulge in the most momentous winter activity *ever?* Hell, even the cranky older brother she'd grown up with had let a few snow angels loose now and then.

"You act like I just told you I've never tied my shoelaces or drunk a glass of milk," he grumbled. "It's just a snow angel."

"*Just* a snow angel?"

Blake offered a shrug.

"And you grew up in Chicago?"

"'Fraid so."

"Well, that's just ridiculous." She planted her gloved hands on her hips. "Get on your back."

"Now *that's* what I'm talking about."

If he didn't look so damn cute with his cheeks flushed from the cold and with that sexy wool hat covering his dark hair, she would've hurled a snowball at him.

"Take your mind out of the sexual gutter, Corwin." She pointed to the snow. "On your back."

Reluctant acceptance filled his gaze. Sighing, he lowered his long, lean body onto the snow, propped his hands behind his head and eyed her expectantly.

A rush of warmth swelled inside her. Had this intense, I-don't-know-how-to-lighten-up FBI agent flopped down on the snowy lawn just because she'd asked or was she imagining it?

Amazed, she quickly lay down on her back beside him before he changed his mind and realized he was indeed anti-fun. "Okay, let's get started."

A carefree sensation slid around in her chest as she and Blake moved their arms and legs in the snow like a couple of silly children. They were both laughing by the time they stood up and examined their respective angels.

"Yours is superior to mine," he complained, brushing snowflakes off his delectable butt. "More graceful."

"Yeah, but yours is really…manly." She tried not to snicker at the result of his effort. While her stretch of snow indeed resembled an angel, Blake's was nothing more than a six-foot area of packed white slush.

"You're a wonderful liar," he replied with a grin. "Just admit it—my angel is pathetic."

"You're right. It's pathetic."

The pale winter sun disappeared behind a patch of clouds, darkening the already overcast sky. A few birds chirped in the distance and she followed the sound, noticing for the first time that the tall brown fence at the far end of the property separated the yard from a wooded area. The gate was open, providing a glimpse of a narrow path covered with snow and shadowed by pine trees.

"What's down there?" she asked curiously.

"A small ravine. Not too spectacular, either. Half a mile and you come out at a neighboring residential street." He frowned. "In fact, the gate should be shut. The blizzard must have blown it open last night."

He marched across the yard to close and lock the gate. "Why do you look so glum?" he teased when he came back.

"I was hoping we could take a walk in the woods. Hey, maybe we can go ice skating in Millennium Park instead?" Her spirits lifted as she remembered the times Beau had taken her there when they were kids.

"I don't think that's a good idea."

His low voice sent her spirits plummeting. What was the matter with her? For a few minutes she'd actually *forgotten* that the Rose Killer was still on the loose and that she was under the protection of the FBI. For God's sake. How could something like that slip her mind?

It was unnerving. How one relaxing morning in the company of this man could make her forget about the murderer still at large.

"Sorry. I wasn't thinking," she said quietly. Brushing snow off the sleeves of her jacket, she trudged toward the back door. "Come on, I'll make us some lunch."

They walked inside, but before they could remove their coats and boots, the doorbell rang. Blake gestured for her to stay in the kitchen, but she followed him out into the hall anyway, both of them leaving a trail of wet snow behind them. "Are you expecting someone?" she asked.

"Rick said he might come by to fill me in on what the team is working on, but he would've called first." His brow furrowed as they neared the door. "Go into the living room, Sam."

This time she didn't argue. She drifted into the other room, seeing from the corner of her eye that Blake had removed his gun from its holster. Keeping the weapon at his side, he opened the door.

She waited for the sound of voices, but all she heard was Blake's faint, "What the…"

Her peripheral vision caught him bending down, reaching for something out of her eyeshot. There was a rustling sound and then Blake cursed and shot to his feet, weapon drawn.

"What's going on?" she blurted out.

"Stay where you are, Samantha." His voice was soft, but when he turned to shoot her an I-mean-it look there was nothing soft about him. His features were all hard angles and sharp planes, lined with…fury, she realized.

It was the rage flashing in his normally shuttered gaze that caused her to ignore his order.

Adrenaline coursing through her blood, she charged to the doorway. Blake was already descending the front steps. He tore across the snow-covered lawn toward the unmarked police car parked at the curb. The *empty* police car.

Oh God, where was Officer Daniels?

Sam's gaze ping-ponged around the front yard but there was no sign of the guard who'd been keeping watch in the car all night.

Her pulse roared in her ears. She slumped against the doorway, unable to process exactly what the hell was going on, and that's when she saw it. The box at her feet. A long, rectangular, gold box.

She bent down, her knees sinking into the wet snow on the doorstep. Her hands were shaking so badly she could barely grasp the edge of the box. She fumbled with it, clawed at it. Opened it.

A wave of nausea shook her equilibrium and sent her falling forward. One hand landed in snow. The other connected with the thorny stem of one very dead rose.

"Daniels!" Blake shouted, keeping both hands on his gun as he stood in the middle of the front yard and searched the street ahead.

Officer Daniels was nowhere in sight, and as much as he wanted to, Blake couldn't go charging through the neighborhood looking for him. He couldn't leave Sam, not when the maniac who'd tried to kill her could still be in the vicinity.

Fury swarmed his gut like an army of wasps. The son of a bitch had been here. He'd waltzed right up to Blake's goddamn *door* to deliver his goddamn *gift*. Where the hell was Daniels?

Blake turned, nearly keeling over when he spotted Sam on the porch. She was on her knees, staring at the dead flowers with a paralyzed expression. The chilled afternoon breeze lifted her dark hair and made it swirl around her face, a beautiful face devoid of any color.

Blake was by her side in an instant. He hauled her to her feet and pushed her toward the front door. He immediately regretted manhandling her, but his rough actions hadn't even sparked a reaction from her. She looked like a deer frozen in the middle of the road while a car careened toward it.

He stood in the open doorway, his gaze shifting from the blackened stems strewn on the doorstep to the disoriented expression on Sam's face. He wanted to destroy the box and its contents, but it was evidence now. Besides, he was afraid if he turned away from Sam she'd collapse. He'd never seen her this agitated, and he knew that when he found him, he was going to strangle the son of a bitch who'd instilled such overwhelming horror in the strongest woman Blake had ever met.

"Sam," he began, but whatever he'd been about to say—he wasn't even sure what—was interrupted by a shout from behind.

Gun in hand, Blake spun around in time to see Officer Daniels dragging a kid in a yellow parka up the front walk.

"Our culprit," Daniels explained angrily, jerking a thumb at the kid.

The boy couldn't have been older than eleven or twelve, and he looked downright terrified by the man with the kung-fu grip on his arm. Blake didn't blame the kid. Officer Glen Daniels was a pretty terrifying man. At least six-five, the cop boasted a shaved head, piercing brown eyes and a scowl that could scare the pants off a Navy SEAL. That's why Blake had found it so hard to believe that someone had gotten past Daniels to deliver those flowers. But apparently he hadn't.

"He tried to take off after leaving the box on the porch," Daniels said, shooting a glare at the young boy, who looked like he was about to wet his pants.

"I didn't do nothin' wrong!" the kid blurted out. He stared at Blake with desperate eyes, begging him to believe him.

Blake sighed, then told Daniels to stay with the kid for a

moment. He moved to the front door and laid a gentle hand on Sam's arm. "You need to go inside."

Wordlessly, she simply nodded and disappeared through the doorway, closing the door softly behind her.

Blake turned around and zeroed in on the kid. "What's your name?"

"Jacob. Jacob Thomson. I live over there." The boy pointed at a white-and-green Victorian across the street.

"Who asked you to deliver these flowers?"

"What flowers?" The boy suddenly noticed the stems strewn across the porch and his freckled face went pale. "I swear, I didn't know what was in the box! The old dude asked me to drop it on the front step and he said he'd give me ten bucks if I did, so I said, Yeah, sure, I'll do it, 'cuz it's, like, easy money, you know? So I did and…" He ran out of steam, coming to an abrupt halt.

Blake was already pulling out his cell phone. He punched in a few numbers and dialed Rick. "Send some patrols to canvas my neighborhood," he said in lieu of greeting. "The bastard's probably miles away by now, but there's always a chance he's still lurking in some bushes."

"What the hell is going on?" Rick demanded.

Blake ignored the question. "I'll call you back."

He shoved the phone into his pocket and returned his attention to the dark-haired boy who'd just delivered a boxful of dead flowers to Blake's doorstep.

"This old dude," Blake said calmly. "Can you describe him? And how old was he exactly?"

Jacob tilted his dark head and rubbed the arm Officer Daniels had finally let go of. "I dunno. He was ancient, like my dad's age or something."

"How old is your father?"

"I dunno. Forty-five?"

Despite himself, Blake fought a smile. To a twelve-year-old, anyone over thirty was apparently *ancient*.

"What did he look like?"

"Um…brown hair, I think. I don't remember what color his eyes were. And he was kinda tall. Not as tall as *him*—" Jacob gave Officer Daniels a dirty look "—but I guess maybe your height?" He gestured to Blake.

"Where did this man approach you?" Blake asked.

"It's a snow day so I didn't have to go to school today, so I was at the end of the street, where there's this, like, monstrous snow-covered hill and I was sliding down it on my sneakers, and the dude just walked up holding that box."

"And told you to deliver it to *this* house specifically?"

"Yeah. He said he couldn't do it himself because his daughter lived there and she wouldn't see him 'cuz he ran out on her when she was a kid, but it's her birthday so he wanted to give her something."

"Did he have a car? A van?"

Young Jacob looked annoyed. "No, I already told you, he just walked up."

The interrogation continued for a few more minutes. Jacob stuck by his story, and it became clear to Blake that the kid was telling the truth. The Rose Killer had simply strolled up to him and given him ten bucks in exchange for making a delivery.

The sheer nerve of it was astounding. The maniac had obviously been very sure of himself, certain of the fact that he could come into this neighborhood and leave it, unnoticed. And he had.

That he now knew where Blake lived was far too unsettling. Rick told him their names had been in the paper, but his address and phone number were unlisted, which meant the Rose Killer had somehow tracked him here.

He furrowed his brows, trying to figure out when it could've happened. He hadn't seen a tail any of the times he'd driven home. More so, he hadn't *felt* a tail. He'd worked in the field long enough to have developed instincts about that sort of thing, and for the life of him he couldn't fathom how someone could've have been following him without him noticing.

Something nagged at the back of his head, a thought even more unsettling than the rest. It was something the profilers and detectives working the case had discarded, but Blake suddenly had to wonder…was this killer a cop?

It seemed unlikely, considering the disarray of the crime scenes, but if the guy wasn't in law enforcement, then at the very least he had tools most civilians lacked. The military term *evade and escape* suddenly came to mind. Had this madman been skilled in evasion techniques? Was his ability to escape into the shadows more than just a case of good luck?

"Uh, dude, can I go now?"

Jacob Thomson's voice jerked him back from his thoughts. He glanced at Jacob, then at Daniels, who still looked pissed off that he'd had to chase the kid through the snow.

"Not just yet," Blake said with a shake of his head. "Right now Officer Daniels here is going to escort you home—are your parents there?"

"My mom is." Jacob paled. "You gotta tell her I didn't do anything wrong!"

"You didn't," Blake assured the kid. "But you're going to need to repeat your statement to Officer Daniels, who will write it all down. And then Officer Daniels will need to speak to your mother."

And warn her to keep you locked up tight, because apparently this street isn't safe anymore, he wanted to add, but quickly tamped down the urge. He didn't want to raise a public panic just yet, not until he spoke to the police super-intendant about the entire situation.

As it was, when he talked to the police chief a few minutes later, Fantana decided not to alert Blake's neighbors and keep it quiet for the meantime, but he'd agreed to up the patrols in the area. After speaking to Rick, and then his supervisor, Blake finally climbed back onto the porch. He left the gold box and dead flowers exactly where they were; the forensics team was on their way to collect the evidence and examine the scene, but Blake knew they wouldn't find anything. The Rose Killer was too smart to leave any incriminating evidence behind, except, of course, for the woman currently inside the house.

The killer had left Sam behind, and as grateful as Blake was that she was alive, he wanted to strangle the bastard who'd once again sparked terror in Samantha Dawson.

Chapter 11

Blake stepped inside and kicked off his boots, then drifted into the living room. Sam was on the couch, her knees lifted up to her chest with her slender arms wrapped around them. Her face was still ashen, and she barely glanced up as he came in.

He hated seeing her like this. She'd gone from being serene and laid-back from an afternoon in the snow, to sad and scared, thanks to a psychopath who was apparently determined to terrorize her.

He watched as she shifted on the sofa. She reached for the red afghan resting on the arm of the couch, gathered the blanket around her legs and met his gaze at last.

Silence stretched between them.

"I'm going to catch him, Sam," he finally said. He didn't know why, but he felt he needed to make things right. To bring the light back into her gorgeous eyes.

She fixed him with a heartbreakingly grim look. "I know you will," she murmured.

After a moment of hesitation, he joined her on the couch. "I know the flowers upset you."

She replied with a humorless laugh. The reaction was so unexpected he didn't know how to respond. Fortunately, he didn't have to, because her next words clarified it all.

"I'm not upset—I'm angry!" she burst out. "He's playing games with me, Blake. He waltzed right into your neighborhood and suckered some poor kid into delivering those disgusting roses!" Her eyes flashed with rage and horror. "What if he'd hurt that boy?"

"But he didn't, thankfully."

"No, of course not." She made a bitter sound. "It's me he wants to hurt."

"I won't let him," he said with conviction.

She released a heavy sigh, the anger in her eyes beginning to dim. Rubbing her forehead, she cast a resigned look in his direction. "It's always there with you, isn't it? This case?"

He frowned. "What do you mean?"

"Earlier, when we were out in the yard…for a moment I was…having fun, I guess." Her chest rose softly as she drew in a long breath then exhaled. "But you didn't forget, did you? The entire time we were outside, the Rose Killer was on your mind, wasn't he?"

He faltered, not sure what to say.

"Tell me why you took this case, Blake."

"I'm not sure what you're getting at," he said roughly.

She leaned into him, moving the blanket so that it covered them both. "Why did you take this case?" she repeated.

"It's my job, Sam."

"It's more than that. You're pushing yourself to the point of exhaustion. You're stressed, you're getting headaches."

"Comes with my line of work," he said flippantly.

"Bull. You're using this case as an excuse. You're hell-bent on finding this guy because it helps you not think about Kate."

His lips tightened. "That's not true."

"Isn't it? Melanie told me Kate died because of a case you were working on."

Shards of stinging pain sliced through him. Why the hell would Melanie have done that?

"You blame yourself for her death, don't you?"

He felt her warm hand move under the blanket. She rested it on his thigh, and he was amazed how her touch could still arouse him when his brain was screaming vile things at him.

"I blame myself because I was at fault," he muttered.

"I don't believe that."

He shrugged her hand away as a violent jolt of fury seared up his spine. Gulping back the acrid taste in his mouth, he curled his hands into tight fists and spoke briskly, as if reciting from a textbook. "Kate was profiling a killer for me. A lead came in and I went after it. She wanted to come along, I let her."

"So?"

Blake twisted around so they were face-to-face. Unwelcome memories swarmed his brain like street litter blowing on the sidewalk. "So I *let* her," he repeated.

Even now, he couldn't fathom how he'd made such an incomprehensible error. Kate had been a desk agent, for God's sake. She'd undergone field training, of course, but she'd never worked outside FBI headquarters in Quantico before. She'd never had to fire a gun at a suspect or don a bulletproof vest or tackle an enraged killer and throw him to the ground.

What the hell had he been thinking, letting her tag along for an arrest?

He said all this to Sam, nearly choking on each word, and the rest of the story wasn't any easier to get out.

"We tracked the perp to an abandoned warehouse outside of Richmond. He popped out of the shadows with a gun. Kate had her back turned to him. I saw him there, raised my own weapon, but I hesitated."

Sam reached for his hand, and this time Blake welcomed her touch. "I had a clear shot of him, but Kate was standing right there and I didn't want her caught in the cross fire. I shouted for her to get down, but she was two seconds too late. He shot her in the back. Twice. He got off his third shot just as my bullet connected with his forehead."

"Blake…I'm sorry."

He closed his eyes, trying to banish the memories to that place in his gut where for more than a year he'd kept them hidden. "I acted like a lover when I should've been a cop," he squeezed out.

"You're human, Blake. And humans make mistakes." She paused. "And who knows, maybe your hesitation wasn't a mistake. Maybe the guy would have shot her anyway."

"And maybe he wouldn't have."

"And maybe if my parents hadn't been workaholics, they wouldn't have been killed by a drunk driver when they'd decided to go into the office on New Year's Eve. There's no point talking about 'ifs' and 'maybes.' Bad things happen."

He drew in a long breath as Sam shifted over and climbed onto his lap. She placed a hand on each of his cheeks and forced him to look at her. He did, and saw the unmistakable compassion swimming in her silvery gaze.

"But good things happen, too, Blake." Her voice was barely

a whisper. "Look at what's happening between us. A week ago I would never have imagined that I could feel anything but fear toward a man. And look at this room—it's dark."

He shot her a questioning look.

"I haven't been in a dark room for six months. At the farmhouse I slept with three lights on, for God's sake. Don't you understand? You've made me stronger, Blake."

"I haven't done a thing," he said quietly. "You're a survivor, right down to the core. You were born strong, Sam."

He tangled his fingers in her silky brown hair and pulled her head down so that their lips were inches apart.

"Hell, you're probably stronger than I am," he whispered before pressing his mouth to hers.

She melted into his kiss. Still cupping his face, she angled his chin to deepen the contact.

Sitting there, with Sam's lush body straddling him, with her firm breasts pressed against his chest and her wet tongue flicking against his, Blake's entire body hardened.

Whether or not they had a future together, he still couldn't fight the attraction he felt for her. That overwhelming need that sucked the oxygen from his lungs and made him weak with arousal.

He deepened the kiss, drove his tongue into her mouth and savored the sweet taste of her. A soft whimper slipped from her throat, making his desire soar like a kite on a windy day. He pushed his hands underneath her sweater and caressed her breasts, while she unzipped his pants and freed him from his boxers. She stroked him gently, and suddenly he couldn't think, couldn't see, couldn't breathe.

He tugged at her jeans and underwear, pulled them down her legs and tossed them onto the floor. Heart thumping, he rolled her onto her back and parted her smooth thighs with his hands. He wanted to touch and explore and drive her as wild as she drove him, but she didn't let him. Instead, she grasped his erection and guided it inside her.

He nearly came right then and there, just from the feel of her wet heat surrounding him and her sighs of pleasure filling his ears.

She moaned. He barely heard it, his blood drumming too loudly in his head. She was so slick, tight, eager. She was exactly what he needed. She was *all* he needed. Swallowing hard, he cupped the soft flesh of her bottom with his hands and lifted her hips, thrusting deeper into her.

Then he withdrew, slightly, aching to go slow but at the same time knowing he was fighting a losing battle. His skin was on fire, his body taut with the desperate need to let go.

"Sam," he started, wanting to apologize, wanting to slow the climax building in his groin. He never got to finish that sentence as he heard her sexy cry, felt her body clench and watched her come apart in his arms.

It was the most incredible sight he'd ever witnessed. The erotic glaze of her eyes, the way she bit down on her bottom lip, her flushed cheeks. She looked wild and wanton and so unbelievably satisfied he felt himself topple right over the edge after her.

With a cry of his own, he let himself go. Succumbed to the intense wave of pleasure that coursed through him, white-hot pleasure as powerful as a category-five hurricane.

He held her tightly, breathing in her intoxicating feminine scent, wanting the moment to last forever.

Forever.

His pleasure wavered at the word. Because forever wasn't an option, was it? The life she'd described to him, the one she wanted to lead when all this was over, was so colossally different from the one he lived. He chased sadistic killers for a living, made himself and those around him a target each time he investigated a new serial homicide.

His heart began to pound. Sam didn't deserve to be surrounded by danger. She was only now starting to put her pain behind her, to gather the shattered pieces of her life. How could he ever ask her to live with the constant threats, the knowledge that the man in her bed might get shot down by a psychopath every time he left the house to do his job?

But dammit, he was tempted to open his heart and his life to her. Once upon a time he'd wanted the same things she did. He and Kate had been engaged and planning their future, and in one split second Kate was gone and a wall had formed around his heart. The wall that Samantha had somehow penetrated.

Christ, whenever she looked at him with those gorgeous silver eyes, whenever her full lips curved into a smile, he was ready to hand his heart to her on a platter. If it weren't so damn disturbing, he would have laughed out loud at the revelation that this curvy model scared him more than any serial killer ever could.

She shifted beneath him, her warm breath tickling his chin.

"You won't be here when this is all over, will you?" she whispered.

Her soft voice, laced with sadness and a startling dose of wisdom, shocked the hell out of him.

He moved so he was on his back and Sam was lying on top of him, and reluctantly met her inquisitive gaze.

"Sam—"

"It's what you were thinking now, wasn't it?"

He swallowed the lump wedged in his throat. "Yes."

With a sigh, Sam disentangled herself from Blake's arms and sat up. She pulled the blanket over her naked lower body.

It was hard to look at him. She probably shouldn't have brought the subject up to begin with, but she'd needed to know.

God, she was an idiot. She'd obviously mistaken sex for something entirely different, been foolish in thinking this affair with Blake would lead to anything more. But it wasn't about sex for her. She'd had her share of lovers, but none of the men she'd been with even compared to Blake Corwin.

It was remarkable, how each time he made love to her it felt like the first time. All her previous experiences faded away, old lovers and past relationships erased from her life's slate, as if Blake were the one man, the only man, who belonged in her bed.

That scared her the most, how he didn't just make her feel like a woman, he made her feel like *his* woman.

"It wouldn't work," he said as if sensing her inner turmoil. "Our lives don't…mesh."

"You don't have to explain, Blake. I understand."

She started to get up, but he held on to her arm. "I need to explain." His features looked strained. "You mean a lot to me, Sam. That's why I'm saying this to you, that's why I have to walk away once this case is over."

She frowned. "I'm sorry, but your reasoning sucks. I mean a lot to you so you're saying goodbye?"

"You don't want to be with a man who chases killers for a living."

Oh jeez. Now he was telling her what she wanted? Men!

"When the Rose Killer is captured, your life will be free of danger," he continued, avoiding her gaze. "But my life…in my life there will always be a threat."

"And you think I can't handle that?"

His voice grew low, desperate. "I *know* you can handle it. I just think you deserve better. You deserve to fix up that old house in Wellstock, build a life with someone whose career doesn't put your life at risk every time he goes to work. You deserve a man who is…whole. And that's not me, Samantha."

Pain pricked her heart, bringing the sting of tears to her eyes. "You know," she finally murmured, "for the longest time I thought the same thing—that I wasn't whole. And guess what, Blake? I'm starting to feel whole now, and it's because of you."

"It's because of you," he corrected. "You're a survivor, remember? And you've suffered so damn much the past year. I don't ever want you to suffer again, sweetheart, even if it means walking away from you."

Funny, that he didn't realize he was making her suffer *now,* by saying these words to her.

"You're not being fair." Her voice cracked so badly that she started to feel pitiful, pleading with him when it was obvious that he didn't intend to change his mind.

She rose from the couch. Even covered by a pair of thick socks, her feet felt cold against the hardwood floor. She quickly put on her panties and jeans. "I get you're used to being in charge, Blake, but you don't get to make decisions for me. For *us.*"

Without meeting her eyes, he pulled his pants and boxers up to his waist, then stood up. His handsome face exuded both frustration and regret.

"I'm making the decision for me," he said hoarsely. Stepping closer, he reached out to trace the outline of her lips with his thumb. "And when you take the time to think about it—*really* think about it—you'll realize I'm doing the right thing."

His hand dropped from her mouth. Slowly, he walked out of the living room.

She stared at his broad back, her eyelids stinging. The right thing? Is that what he considered ripping her heart right out of her chest and crushing it between his fingers?

She wanted to curse with anger and disappointment. Whatever he thought he was doing by pushing her away, whatever he thought she'd gain from him walking away from her—there was absolutely nothing *right* about it.

She hesitated, wanting to run after him and tell him he was being a fool, but she kept herself rooted in place. No, she wasn't going to chase after him. She wasn't going to try to change his mind. Whether or not this affair with Blake went any further, she needed to take care of herself first. She was just now putting the pieces of her life back together, and she wasn't about to hinder her progress by becoming a clingy and desperate woman who couldn't live without a man.

If Blake wanted her, he was going to have to come and get her.

"Sam?"

He was standing in the doorway again, and a balloon of hope rose in her chest before she could stop it. He was back. He'd realized he was acting like an idiot and that maybe whatever it was between them really was worth pursuing and—

"Elaine's on the phone."

The balloon burst, little pieces of hope sinking and settling in the pit of her stomach like jagged little rocks.

Of course he wouldn't change his mind. The master of control never doubted his decisions after he'd made them, no matter how unfair and *unnecessary* they were.

Without a word, she walked up and accepted the cordless phone from his hands, then brushed past him without sparing him a backward glance.

"Hey, hon, what's going on?" she said into the receiver

as she climbed the stairs with a heavy heart and headed for the guest room.

She'd moved her things into Blake's bedroom yesterday, but she had no intention of spending the night there tonight. Trying not to cry, she sank onto the bed and leaned back against the headboard.

"I just spoke to Dr. Darwitz," came Elaine's soft voice, followed by a sniffle. "He sent some pictures, you know, of my…my scars…to the plastic surgeon at CGH and he heard back from him today."

Sam tried not to cringe as she remembered the countless bandages on Elaine's small body. Nausea scampered up her throat but she swallowed it down, refusing to let Elaine hear any sympathy or pity in her voice. Support. That's all she would offer this courageous young woman.

"What did he say?" she asked gently.

"He's willing to perform the surgery. But he said there could be residual scarring. Especially on my breasts."

A strangled sob sounded from the other end of the line.

"Hey, don't cry, honey. That's good news, isn't it?"

"Didn't you hear me? He can't get rid of them completely, Sam!"

"Then maybe you have to take what you can get," she replied quietly. "If you want the surgery, accept the limitations. *Do* you want the surgery?"

Silence. Stretching out so long that Sam thought Elaine might have hung up. She opened her mouth to speak but another sob tore through the extension, laced with such misery that tears stung Sam's eyes. God, this poor girl. This poor, innocent girl who'd done nothing wrong except go into work on the day a madman decided to show up. It wasn't fair. It was so beyond fair that Sam suddenly felt like hitting someone, throwing something, anything to release the tornado of anger spinning inside her.

"I know the idea that you'll always have some scars is troubling," she finally said, swallowing back the rage bubbling in her throat. Her heart ached for the twenty-three-year-old who, at the moment, was locked up in a safe house so a killer couldn't find her. "But Elaine, if the surgeon can make even one scar disappear, I think you should do it, honey."

"What about you?" was Elaine's shaky reply.

Sam faltered. "What about me?"

"Are you getting yours removed?"

"I…don't know." She chewed on the inside of her cheek.

"Doesn't it make you feel ugly?" Elaine burst out. "Aren't you scared that if you show it to someone, he'll laugh at you and be repulsed?"

Sam hesitated. Blake's voice suddenly drifted into her head, the quiet words he'd uttered when they'd first made love. *You've got a war wound.*

He hadn't been repulsed by the scar. He said it impressed him, that it showed her strength.

"I'm not scared," she answered, shrugging off the troubling thought. "If someone wants to laugh at me, or run away in horror, let him. We're survivors, honey. And if we survived the wrath of a madman, we sure as hell can survive the rejection of a person who can't look beneath the surface."

Another silence dragged between them, until Elaine finally made a desperate, strangled sound and whispered, "I'm not a survivor, Sam. I'm a victim. I'll never be anything else."

"Don't say that! Elaine, please, you need to know that you'll get through this. You'll—"

The assurances fell on deaf ears. Elaine had already hung up.

Sam clutched the phone between trembling fingers. She

wanted to run downstairs and force Blake to take her to that safe house. She wanted to pull that sad, suffering girl into her arms and make the pain go away. But she couldn't. Blake wasn't about to drive her to Indiana, and she knew Elaine wouldn't accept the offer of comfort anyway. For Elaine, comfort would come later. Comfort would come the morning she opened her eyes and didn't remember what happened to her, the day she looked into the mirror and didn't see a multitude of scars branded into her body.

The tears finally started to fall, streaming down her cheeks until her eyes felt swollen and her skin was raw. She yearned to go downstairs and find warmth and solace in Blake's arms, but tonight it had become clear that he wasn't emotionally available to her. A part of her would forever be grateful to him, for helping her reclaim her womanhood, for showing her that a man's touch could evoke something other than fear inside her. But a physical connection wasn't enough for her.

She wanted all the things she'd almost lost because of the attack. Love. Passion. Companionship. Family.

Blake couldn't give her that.

No, Blake *wouldn't* give her that.

And as devastating as it was, better he'd told her sooner than later. Better he'd told her before she did something foolish.

Like fall in love with him.

"I made some coffee," Blake said when Sam walked into the kitchen the next morning. Even to his own ears his voice sounded overly cheerful, as if a friendly tone and a pleasant smile could erase what had happened between them last night.

"Thanks." She didn't return the smile. Just rounded the counter and poured herself some coffee.

She wore a black turtleneck that hugged her full breasts and a pair of tight black jeans that made her long legs seem endless. The all-black getup made her appear incredibly sophisticated. With it she looked like she belonged on a sidewalk in Manhattan, with a steaming Starbucks cup in a gloved hand as she swayed those sexy hips over to a modeling session. Hands down she was the most beautiful woman he'd ever laid eyes on, and the sight of her, distant gray eyes and all, sent doubt spiraling through him.

The words he'd said to her yesterday circled his brain like a hungry turkey vulture and made him crazy with uncertainty. It was for the best, wasn't it? Telling Sam their affair would have to end was something that needed to be done. And he'd meant what he said. She deserved far more than he could give her.

However, that didn't stop his chest from feeling like it had been scraped raw, or his throat from clogging when he looked at her achingly gorgeous face and stared at those lush lips he wanted more than anything to kiss.

She'd slept in the guest room last night. He knew it shouldn't bother him, but it did. He wished they'd shared the same bed, wished he could've made love to her again and held her as she'd slept.

What he wished the most was that he could give her the life she deserved, the life she'd *earned*.

But he couldn't. He had no plans to quit his job, and even if he were willing to allow Sam to live with the risks his career posed, he hadn't been lying when he told her he didn't feel whole. He'd taken the Rose Killer case to make him forget about Kate's death, but he hadn't forgotten. It wasn't fair to force Sam to share that burden with him. Letting go of the guilt was something he needed to do alone.

"So what's on the agenda for today?" Sam asked, her tone

both cool and controlled. "Do you have that task force meeting to go to?"

He nodded. "Fantana's team has been working overtime to follow up on the possible florist link. I haven't heard from Rick, but I'm hoping they made some headway."

On cue, his cell phone began to chirp.

Sam raised a brow. "Maybe they have."

He flipped open the phone, saw Rick's number on the screen, and answered. "Please tell me we've got a lead."

Rick's pause was so brief nobody else would've read anything into it, but Blake knew his partner well and that tiny pause immediately caused his features to strain. "What's going on?"

Rick spoke.

Blake listened.

He felt the blood slowly drain out of his face, knew his complexion must have gone pale, and he quickly turned away so Sam wouldn't see it.

He didn't turn fast enough. The second he hung up the phone Sam was in front of him, coffee abandoned, expression creased with worry. "What happened?" she demanded.

He fought the nausea. Swallowed against it. Inhaled deeply.

He didn't have to tell her. Looking at her concerned face, he knew he could spare her from this. Shrug it off, assure her all was well in the world, and allow her to continue healing without the added burden. How many more burdens would she able to carry? He'd seen how the flower delivery had shaken her up, and this… Christ, this would send her tumbling right over the edge.

She didn't need to hear it. It didn't affect her. It didn't *have* to affect her.

It affects her, you insensitive ass!

He almost keeled over at the sound of Kate's voice in his head.

He tried to shut out the unwelcome intrusion. He couldn't think about Kate right now. He couldn't listen to her reprimand him from the goddamn grave.

And yet his conscience refused to let him ignore—both Kate and the truth he was considering withholding from Sam. Because Kate was right. What Rick had just told him affected Sam and he would be buying a one-way ticket to hell if he kept it from her.

"Blake...you're scaring me," she murmured.

He raked his fingers through his hair and took another breath. "I'm sorry. I wasn't trying to scare you. Sam..." Another breath. The oxygen burned right down to his lungs. "Elaine Woodman killed herself."

Chapter 12

The world promptly crumbled beneath Sam's feet. She staggered forward, right into Blake's solid chest, right into a pair of warm arms that instantly wrapped around her and pulled her close. He was saying something to her, but the words were muffled by the dull roar of her pulse in her ears.

"Is this a joke?" She pressed her palms to his chest and pushed him away. Then she was stumbling backward, edging toward the doorway as if running would make it all go away. "Is this some kind of sick, insensitive joke?"

He shook his head.

She shook her head right back. "No. *No*. You're lying."

Pain filled his amber-colored eyes. "I'm sorry, Sam. Rick just heard from Mel. She was staying with Elaine at the safe house, and she—" His Adam's apple bobbed as he swallowed. "She found her about twenty minutes ago."

"She's lying." The vehemence in her tone terrified her. Did

that shrill, enraged voice belong to her? "Elaine would never do that. She wouldn't kill herself. She's twenty-three years old, for God's sake! And she…she…"

It suddenly became increasingly difficult to breathe. Her heart was pounding so hard her ribs were beginning to hurt, her chest felt like it would cave in any second, and her eyes were stinging so badly she couldn't even see Blake anymore.

She could hear him, though. And God, how she wished she could shut out that calm, almost mechanical voice he was using.

"Melanie found her in the bedroom. She used a telephone cord to…to hang herself." Now he was cool and efficient. "She left a note."

Sam stared at him, horrified. Wanting to slap that professional expression off his face, but her hands were shaking so wildly she couldn't even lift them to wipe the tears that poured down her cheeks. So instead of hitting him, she exploded.

"What is the matter with you?" She gasped for air. "How can you just stand there like a robot and tell me Elaine *hanged herself* like you're reciting a passage from a goddamn textbook? Do you even *care* that she's dead? Do you?"

For a moment he looked stunned. Then a flash of fire erupted in his eyes. Every feature on his face tightened, his shoulders stiffened, his hands curled into fists.

"Of course I care," he hissed out. "It tears me up inside knowing that innocent girl took her own life, that she was so goddamn traumatized by what that maniac did to her that she didn't feel it was worth living. It tears me up."

He finished with a ragged groan, and a wave of guilt slammed into her as she saw the pure anguish flashing on his face. Oh, God. Why had she said those hurtful things? She knew Blake wasn't a robot, she knew how deeply he cared about the victims whose killer he was chasing.

"I'm sorry," she managed to whisper. "I'm…sorry."

He was by her side again in an instant. This time he didn't draw her into his arms, but he did reach out and lace his fingers through hers. "I know how much this must hurt. I know you and Elaine connected and that you cared about her."

She clamped her lips together to keep a sob from slipping out. Taking a long breath, she opened her mouth and said, "You said there was a note. What did it say?"

The hesitation on his face caused her to shrug her hand away. "It's…not important," he said roughly.

"Like hell it isn't! What did it say, Blake?"

He was quiet for so long she thought he wasn't going to answer. But then he opened his mouth and told her, and suddenly she wished he hadn't.

Her throat squeezed. "Say it again," she choked out.

"Sam—"

"*Again.*"

"The note said, 'I'm not a survivor. I'm not strong like you.'" He hurried on. "It doesn't mean she addressed it to you. It could have been written to anyone."

Sick. She was going to be sick. Spinning on her heels, she tore out of the kitchen and stumbled into the small bathroom in the hall, where she dropped to her knees and emptied the guilt and horror from her stomach. And when there was nothing left, she just sat there and cried. Cried and cursed and cried some more until the guilt turned to anger and the anger to sheer rage.

She cleaned up, then left the bathroom. Blake was waiting for her in the hallway, his gaze concerned, but she didn't see him. All she saw was the red haze of fury before her eyes.

"I'm going to kill him," she whispered.

"Let's go and sit down so we could talk about—"

"I don't want to sit down! I'm going to kill that son of a bitch, Blake!" She released a shaky breath. "He did this to her. *He* did it, and I'm not going to rest until I watch him die."

The concern on his face deepened, and she knew she must look and sound like a crazy person right now. Her face was stained with tears, her hair had fallen out of the loose bun she'd twisted it in and was now sticking to her cheeks and eyes. She'd never experienced wrath like this before— blinding, hot, all-consuming. Although she tried not to, she couldn't stop picturing Elaine, how she must have looked when Melanie Barnes had found her, how hopeless and scared she must have felt when she decided to take her own life.

Had she done it right after they'd gotten off the phone last night? Or had she woken up this morning and known, just *known,* that she couldn't keep going?

The answer to either of those questions didn't matter. Nothing mattered except that the man who'd almost killed Sam had claimed another victim.

"Sam, you need to calm down," Blake said softly. "I know this hurts, but—"

"But you'd prefer I bury the hurt deep inside?" she shot back. "That is your standard operating procedure, isn't it?"

Shock filled his features, yet he didn't argue. They both knew she was right, but being right didn't make her feel one bit better. From the moment she'd met him, she'd sensed that Blake was closed off, that his unwavering control and the cool mask he liked to wear were his way of dealing with the pain in his life. She understood, because, hell, hadn't she been doing the same thing these past six months? Putting on an in- different front and pretending she wasn't hurting anymore?

Well, she was sick of doing it, and she was sick of watching Blake pretend. How could he make love to her as if she were the only woman in the world who mattered and then tell her in that irritatingly professional voice that their relationship wouldn't go any further?

God help her, but she wanted to be with this man, no matter how infuriating he could be and no matter how many times he tried convincing her that he wasn't right for her. And maybe they *were* all wrong for each other, maybe this entire crazy situation was clouding her judgment, but at the moment she didn't give a damn.

She was *angry*. At Blake. At Elaine. At the Rose Killer. And she wasn't about to pretend to be anything *but* angry.

"You weren't being fair last night," she found herself bursting out.

Discomfort practically seeped from his pores. He raked one hand through his dark hair then rubbed his forehead. "Let's not do this right now, Sam."

"No, *let's*." She frowned. "You can't just decide you don't want me anymore and then expect me to smile and laugh and act like it doesn't matter."

"You think I don't want you?" He laughed harshly. "God, Sam, I want you so bad it's driving me crazy! I've been walking around hot for you from the day we met—and you think I don't know how wrong that is? You're a witness, and a victim—"

"I'm a woman!" she roared. Her cheeks burned with insult. "Deal with it, Blake, and quit hiding behind excuses and convoluted notions about me deserving better." She took a calming breath. "You can't tell me you don't see what's happening between us."

His jaw tensed. "Sex. That's what happened between us."

She stared at him in disbelief. "You honestly believe that's all it is?" When he didn't answer, she curled her hands into fists and stalked past him, heading for the stairs. "You're a son of a bitch, Blake Corwin."

She'd only taken two steps when his warm hand grasped her arm. She spun around. From her perch on the staircase she was a good foot taller than he was and she looked down at him with daggers in her eyes.

"I'm sorry. Goddammit, you're right, I didn't mean it," he squeezed out.

The pain flickering in his whiskey eyes was so visceral that her gaze softened, along with her body. A shaky breath rolled out of her chest and before she could second-guess herself she touched his jaw and gently trailed her fingers across it. "It's okay," she said with a sigh.

"No, it's not." He made a strangled sound and then his arms were wrapping around her. Her higher position offered a strange sense of power, as Blake nestled his face against her breasts, his silky brown hair tickling the bottom of her chin.

She ran her fingers through that gorgeous hair and breathed in the scent of his woodsy shampoo. Something inside her began to stir and the warmth spreading across her skin shocked the hell out of her. God, this wasn't the time to want this.

"It's more than sex for me," he said, his warm breath fanning over her collarbone and sizzling right through the ribbed fabric of her turtleneck. "If it were, I wouldn't be so damn terrified right now."

He lifted his head and the kaleidoscope of emotions swirling in his eyes sucked the breath right out of her lungs. She saw his passion and desire, his admiration and respect, and God help her, she saw *love*. He might never say the words aloud, but she saw the love in his eyes, so naked and strong that she nearly keeled over from the force of it.

She knew he probably wouldn't change his mind—he

honestly believed that she deserved a life that couldn't be threatened by him or his job—but at the moment it didn't matter. Blake Corwin cared for her more than he was willing to admit, he *loved* her, and it was probably time to face the fact that she loved him, too.

"Sam?"

She blinked, found him looking up at her with those serious brown eyes. Wondered if he sensed—and understood—the current of emotions crackling between them.

"I care about you, you know," he said thickly. He swallowed before continuing. "I care a lot. But everything I said last night still—"

She silenced him by placing her finger on his lips. "Please. Don't say it again. Not now."

His pained expression told her he wasn't going to drop it, so this time she shut him up with a kiss.

She thought he would resist, but he surprised her. The urgency of his response fueled her own passion, and when he slipped his tongue into her mouth she let out a low moan and tangled her fingers in his hair.

Their mouths fused, tongues dueled. Heat speared her body, arousal thudded in her veins, and she was breathless when she finally broke the kiss and reached for the hem of her turtleneck.

"This probably isn't a good idea," he murmured huskily, but his eyes were devouring every inch of flesh she revealed.

"I don't care," she murmured back.

She pulled the shirt over her head and tossed it over the railing before fumbling with the button on her jeans. Then she was standing over him, wearing nothing but a silk baby-blue bra and white bikini panties.

Blake's hot gaze swept over her skin and set it on fire. But he didn't touch her.

"Please." A pleading note to her voice. God, was he going to make her beg?

She didn't have to because his hands were suddenly on her body and his tongue was sliding through her lips again. He moved one hand between her legs and she gasped, the provocative touch making her shake with need. With a soft groan, he pulled her down. Lying across the cool wooden stairs wasn't the most comfortable position she would've chosen, but soon her surroundings faded away and all she could focus on was Blake.

His mouth and tongue were everywhere. On her lips. Her neck. Her breasts. He kissed a pebbled nipple through her bra but didn't linger, just dragged his warm mouth down to her navel, circled her belly button with his tongue and then licked along her inner thigh. When he pressed his mouth to her panties she gave a wild cry that filled the brightly lit entrance.

The intimate kisses were almost too much to bear, too teasing, too *not enough*. She wanted his mouth on her flesh, on that throbbing spot that ached for his touch, but she wanted him inside her more. And he sensed it, because after one last soft kiss to her core, he slid up her body, pulling off his shirt on his way up.

His chest was hot to the touch, his heart thudding against her tingling breasts as their bodies met. He kissed her again, cupping one breast with his hand while rummaging in his pocket with the other. Impatience bellowed in her ears as she waited for him, as she felt him fumble with his zipper and sheath himself with a condom.

And then finally, *finally,* his tip brushed over her opening. She arched her hips, trying to draw him in, but he pulled back.

The indecision in his eyes brought a curse to her lips. "No, don't stop now," she whispered. "Please."

The muscles of his chest were so taut it was obvious he was fighting his own restraint. "Last night…"

"Last night you told me you won't be here for me when this is all over." She swallowed hard. "Well, fine, Blake, just be here for me *now.*"

Before he could reply, or argue, or reject her, she reached between them, grasped his erection and brought it inside her.

He groaned, and pleasure rocketed through her. Her body stretched to accommodate him, but it was a spectacular sensation. He belonged here, buried inside, and they both knew it as he slowly began to move.

The stairs dug into her back but she didn't care. She barely felt the irritating pain, only the rapture Blake gave her. His thrusts were hurried, lacking finesse or rhythm as he plunged into her, filling her then retreating, then filling her again without abandon.

"I won't last long," he choked out.

"Good. Neither will I," she murmured back.

Pleasure tightened her body, building and rising until the sensations were almost unbearable. The first tremors of orgasm rippled inside her, but she fought them, watching Blake's heavy-lidded eyes, waiting, needing to come apart only when he did.

One more deep thrust and he toppled over the edge, groaning her name as his climax shuddered through him.

She let herself go.

Her body shattered, consumed by ecstasy so intense she could hardly breathe. Shards of light danced in front of her eyes and she gasped for air, wrapping her legs around Blake's firm buttocks to ride out the body-numbing sensations.

Time passed. Seconds. Minutes. It could have been hours for all she knew. When she finally crashed down to earth she found Blake smiling at her, a faint satisfied smile that told her he'd felt everything she had.

She wanted to thank him for making her feel this way. Desirable and brave and whole.

She wanted to tell him she loved him.

Yet she couldn't. Giving her body to this man had been hard enough, but giving him her heart, knowing he might hand it right back? No. She wasn't *that* brave.

So she simply pressed her face against his damp chest, breathed in his soapy masculine scent, wrapped her arms around his neck.

And held on for as long as she could.

Blake waited for the large conference room the Rose Killer task force was working out of to fill up with the officers involved in the case. Superintendent Jake Fantana stood at the head of the table, an annoyed let's-get-down-to-business look in his pale-blue eyes. Fantana was six-three, bulky as hell, and could make any man cower in his presence, even without the pissed-off daggers in his gaze.

"Let's get started," Fantana barked.

The detectives who'd worked the case for almost a year now lowered themselves into various chairs. A young female officer moved away from one of the large bulletin boards that had been set up in the room and quickly scurried toward a chair.

Blake's gaze strayed to one particular bulletin board, the one reserved for the fourth victim—Sam. A black-and-white photograph of her was tacked onto the board. Her expression held the hint of a smile and seeing it made Blake's chest tighten. The way she was smiling in that picture—it almost reminded him of Kate, that sassy little tilt of the mouth, the stubborn curve of the lips. And yet there was something very un-Kate-like about that smile.

From the start, Sam had reminded him of the woman he'd lost, but he was starting to notice the differences between the two. Like Sam, Kate had been headstrong, tough and too damn intelligent for her own good. But Kate had also been serious. She'd rarely laughed, was exasperatingly conservative at times, never called him on his flaws or misdeeds. Kate wouldn't have rolled around in the snow with him, or forced him to show emotion over Elaine Woodman's senseless death.

No, that was all Sam. Sam, with her melodic laughter and that air of confidence she was only now starting to display. She'd changed since they'd met. No longer wary, no longer fearful. Or perhaps she hadn't changed so much as simply reverted back to the woman she'd been before the attack.

And dammit, but he *liked* that woman. He liked seeing her grow stronger, laughing, taking control of her body again. Hell, he even liked when she yelled at him. Except for his mother, no one in his life ever challenged him. He knew he could be excessively intense, as Kate had been. He knew he tended to shut down when a situation got too emotional, and the women in his life had always let him get away with it.

But Sam…she *forced* him to feel. *Forced* him to laugh.

He might be bad for her, but goddammit, she was good for *him*. And that just made his decision to walk away from her a million times worse.

"There have been some new developments," Fantana announced.

Blake lifted his head at the chief's remark, forcing his personal issues out of his head. He hoped this task force meeting would distract him from his conflicting emotions and finally provide new insight into this case. Rick had phoned earlier and hinted that one of the detectives had dug up something, but Blake hadn't been able to question his partner about it. He'd been too busy briefing John Perkins, the officer who'd come to the house to stay with Sam until the meeting ended.

Had he been too hard on the young cop when he'd told him to guard Sam with his life or else?

Yeah, that *or else* had probably been harsher than necessary. But dammit, leaving her, even for a few hours, was unbearable.

Yet you plan on doing precisely that once the case is closed.

He ignored the irksome voice and focused on the meeting.

Rick started off. "We tracked down the designer who'd sent flowers to Samantha Dawson and he gave us the name of the florist his secretary had used. It was the Grant Flower Shoppe, located near Wicker Park." Rick leaned back in his chair. "I'll let Detective Hodges take it from there."

Burt Hodges glanced down at a sheet of paper on the table and pushed his reading glasses onto a nose far too large for his angular face. "I had a chat with the store manager, who was kind enough to grant us access to the computer records. Candace Lindley, our first victim, received a flower arrangement from that florist the day she died. Same goes for Roberta Diaz and Diana Barrett. Samantha Dawson, however, received her arrangement—" Hodges scanned the paper "—a week before the attack on her."

"And Elaine Woodman?" Blake prompted, his fingers tightening over the tabletop. Just saying Elaine's name out loud brought a rush of guilt to his gut. A part of him still believed her suicide could have been prevented. That *he* could have prevented it, if only he'd caught this maniac sooner.

"It was harder to connect her with the Grant Flower Shoppe, but we finally hit pay dirt when the store manager conducted an address search after Elaine's name never showed up on the receiver list. A coworker of hers received two dozen red roses the day Elaine was abducted. The woman worked in the cubicle next to Elaine's."

"Our guy could have seen Elaine when he was making that delivery," Melanie Barnes mused, running her hands through her short blond hair.

"So aside from all our vics being slender brunettes, this flower angle is the only thread connecting the five women," Rick said, taking the lead again. "So we cross-referenced the deliveries with the person who made them." A slight smile crossed his lips. "We came up with a name."

Blake's throat grew dry. "Who?"

"Francis Grant, the owner."

There was a low murmur from some of the detectives. Frowning, Blake glanced at his partner. "Since when does the store owner make deliveries?"

"The manager said Grant helps out when one of his workers calls in sick. Apparently he's a hands-on kind of guy."

"I'll bet he is," Fantana said grimly. "As it is now, Francis Grant's name is at the top of our suspect list."

"It's the *only* name on our suspect list," one of the detectives quipped ruefully.

Fantana silenced the kidder with a look. "So what have we managed to dig up on Grant?"

Hodges spoke up. "White male, forty-one years old. He inherited the flower shop from his father, been running it for twenty years, and lives in a brownstone near the store. It was deserted when our guys went over there."

Blake plucked a random paper clip from the table and began snapping it between his fingers, his excitement rising at each new development. They were onto something here, close to cracking this case right open. "Any other real estate?" he asked.

Hodges shook his head. "Nothing we've been able to uncover."

"What about the guy's history?" Fantana demanded.

"Military," Hodges answered.

Blake's head jerked up. "Military? You're sure about that?"

Hodges nodded. "He enlisted in the army when he was eighteen, left when he was twenty-one, honorable discharge." Some more papers were shuffled. "He fought in the Gulf, part of Desert Storm, actually. Didn't leave because of an injury, as far as we know, but we're trying to get his full record. Army's sending it over."

Goddamn military. The adrenaline coursing through Blake's blood made his fingers tingle. Everything became clearer now—why he hadn't spotted a tail on him, how the guy continued to evade capture and waltz around as if he wore a cloak of invisibility. The Rose Killer had been *trained* to be invisible. Trained to kill. The army had taught him well.

Obviously a little *too* well.

"Oh," Hodges added, "and we found a death certificate for a woman we believe was his wife. Anne Grant, deceased as of…" Hodges looked at his file again and read off a date.

Blake sucked in a breath. Anne Grant had died two weeks before the first murder. Was that the trigger they'd been looking for?

"Cause of death?" Melanie asked, curious.

Hodges could barely conceal his pleased smile. "Get this— suicide. Anne Grant slit her own wrists."

Blake lifted one wary brow. "You sure Grant didn't do her in and we're looking at six victims instead of five?"

Hodges's smile faded. "We're not sure yet. Ruiz is getting a warrant to access the hospital records. We'll know soon. But the slitting of the wrists—that's important, right?"

Seeing the distressed glimmer in the detective's eyes, Blake nodded. "Of course it is."

"Good work, Hodges," Fantana boomed. "Keep digging, find out everything you can about this man. Samson, I want you to put an APB out on him. Now."

The curly-haired female detective nodded and bounced out of her chair. "I'm on it."

"You three," Fantana barked, pointing to the officers on his left, "set up surveillance on Grant's house and flower shop. If he makes an appearance, grab him."

"Yes, sir."

Three more bodies hurried out of the conference room as Fantana continued to bark out orders at his team. There was electricity in the air that hadn't been there since that first murder, when the evidence had been fresh, the morale high.

Suddenly the case was alive again, and for the first time in weeks—no, months—the ache in Blake's temples subsided.

Chapter 13

"Do you want another cup of coffee?" Sam asked the officer sitting at Blake's kitchen table.

John Perkins glanced up with a smile. He had very nice eyes, she realized. They were almost as dark as his skin, and exuded warmth and sincerity that made her feel at ease. "No thank you, Miss Dawson."

"Are you hungry? I could fix something for you."

He chuckled. "Why don't you sit down, instead? You're making me dizzy, pacing back and forth like that."

Was she pacing? She hadn't noticed. But she wasn't surprised, and she knew exactly who to blame for her incessant restlessness. Blake Corwin and his too-honorable-for-his-own-good attitude.

It riled her that he just assumed he knew what was best for her. Her parents had done the same thing. They'd told her from birth that she was destined to be a lawyer, without ever asking her if she was even interested in the law or giving her any choice in the matter.

Blake wasn't giving her a choice, either. He'd decided that she'd be better off without him and to hell with what she felt about the subject.

And dammit, but she knew precisely how she felt about it.

She didn't want to say goodbye to Blake Corwin. Not by a long shot. She was definitely planning to talk to him about it when he got home from that meeting. He would not push her away this time. She'd fought for her life, thanks to the Rose Killer, but when that psychopath was finally caught she would be fighting for something else.

The man she loved.

She didn't care how many excuses Blake gave her. She didn't care that he was irritatingly serious, or that he turned into stone whenever something threatened his precious control. Kate's death had hit him hard, but Sam was going to be there for him. She was going to help him heal, the way he'd helped her.

To hell with his honorable intentions.

"All right, you're evidently not going to stop pacing," Officer Perkins said with a cheerful smile. "So how about we distract ourselves? Does Agent Corwin have any games in the house? Monopoly? Maybe a deck of cards?"

"We could look," she said, the idea of distracting herself with a game becoming more and more appealing. "Cards would be nice."

"You sure about that? I play a mean game of Texas Hold 'Em."

She grinned. "So do I, buddy, so do I."

Smiling, Perkins stood up. "I'll check the living room." He took two steps to the doorway but halted when the cell phone clipped to his belt began to ring. He quickly lifted it to his ear.

"Perkins," he said into the phone. A frown reached his lips. "Now? Does Agent Corwin know about this?"

Her pulse sped up as his frown deepened. She wished she could hear what was being said at the other end. From Perkins's grim expression, it didn't sound good.

"I understand…yes, sir…I'm on my way." Perkins switched off the phone and turned to her with a look that held both worry and promise. "That was Burt Hodges, one of the senior detectives working your case," he began. "You're being moved to a safe house."

Surprise jolted into her. "Now?"

"I'm afraid so." Perkins was already walking toward the front hallway to grab his coat from the hook by the door. "An officer named Paul Benson is on his way to pick you up."

"What? Why aren't you taking me?"

He slipped into his jacket, his expression now hard. "There's been a break in the case. I'm needed at the station."

Hope spurted in her chest like lava from a long-dormant volcano. "They caught him?"

Perkins reached out and touched her arm. "As far as I know, not yet. But we're close. For your own protection, you can't be in the city right now. Agent Corwin gave the order himself."

She was annoyed. Of course Blake gave the order. She knew he genuinely wanted to keep her safe, but there was definitely more behind the request to ship her off. Earlier she'd made it clear that she wanted to discuss their relationship, even if he wouldn't admit they had one. This was his way of sidestepping the discussion, forcing her into hiding so he didn't have to face everything he was feeling for her.

"Officer Daniels is right outside," Perkins said gently, obviously mistaking her expression for worry rather than the irritation it was. "You're not to go anywhere until Officer Benson arrives to escort you."

"Yes, sir."

His eyes crinkled affectionately. "I'm sorry we couldn't find a deck of cards. I would have enjoyed beating you in Hold 'Em."

"Yeah, in your dreams."

He was laughing as he left the house. Before she closed the door, she gave a little wave to Daniels, who was sitting in his unmarked patrol car, looking scary as usual. He waved back but didn't smile.

She drifted back into the kitchen to make a quick cup of coffee before she had to leave. It took ten minutes for the fresh pot to brew, and just as she was pouring herself a cup, the doorbell rang. Damn. Abandoning the coffee, she headed for the hall, wondering if she should pack a bag. Perkins hadn't told her to, so she assumed that wherever she went, she'd be provided for.

The idea that Blake could be handcuffing the Rose Killer at this exact moment sent a thrill of relief sliding into her. Was the nightmare finally over?

The doorbell rang again, and she quickened her pace, then paused when she reached the front hall. There was a small notepad sitting on the credenza next to the hall closet, and she moved toward it. After a second of hesitation, she scrawled a quick note on the pad, placed the paper where Blake would be sure to see it, then grabbed her coat and slipped it on.

She knew Blake would come to the safe house the moment the Rose Killer was hauled away, but in case he came home first, she wanted him to know that he couldn't avoid the talk they needed to have. Whether he liked it or not, she had no intention of letting him walk away from her that easily.

"Sorry, I was just getting ready," she said as she opened the front door.

The officer on the porch responded with a patient smile. "No worries." He quickly flashed her his badge. "I'm Officer Paul Benson. I'll be escorting you to the location Agent Corwin specified."

Benson seemed pleasant enough. His looks were on the plain side, brown hair, brown eyes, nondescript features. He was also on the thin side. The crisp, white shirt that was part of his uniform hung loosely over his chest, and his black pants seemed ill-fitting. She wondered if he'd lost some weight recently, but didn't ask. Definitely not something you brought up during a first meeting.

"Ready to go?" Benson asked.

"Let me just set the alarm." She didn't know why she bothered, considering that the threat of the Rose Killer was obviously being taken care of elsewhere.

A flicker of panic hit her as she realized that Blake could very well be dealing with that threat right now. What if he got hurt? What if the Rose Killer shot Blake while trying to escape?

She quickly swallowed back the sticky fear in her throat, saying a silent prayer as she zipped up her coat and followed Benson down the porch steps.

Blake would be okay. He was a trained professional, and she had to trust that he could take care of himself.

Benson led her to the police cruiser parked in the driveway and opened the passenger door for her. With a brisk wave at the other car by the curb, he slid into the driver's side and started the engine.

"It shouldn't take us long to reach our destination," Benson said conversationally as he backed out of the snow-covered driveway.

The snowplows had already cleared most of Blake's street, but evidence of the blizzard still remained in the form of massive snowbanks and some slippery patches on the asphalt. Benson kept to the speed limit, leaving Blake's neighborhood and heading toward Chicago's Loop district.

Sam's hands began to shake as her escort turned onto the highway ramp. She didn't feel right leaving the city behind. Leaving Blake behind.

He'll be okay.

She held on to that reassuring thought, but it was hard to relax, knowing that Blake could be in danger right at this moment.

Though she didn't want to admit it, she suddenly understood where he'd been coming from when he'd explained why he didn't want her in his life. He was a federal agent, and she knew that if she chose to be with him, she'd constantly worry about his safety. If he was late, she'd panic. If he took on a particularly dangerous case, she'd be scared 24/7.

And yet the worry and panic and fear didn't seem to matter in the grand scheme of things. She could deal with it, as long as it meant waking up every morning to one of Blake Corwin's rare smiles and falling asleep encircled by those strong arms every night.

"So how long have you been with the department?" she asked her companion, suddenly needing the contact, the diversion. There was something very familiar about him, but Sam couldn't quite put her finger on where she'd seen him before.

Benson shot her an enigmatic smile. "Not long. I'm fairly new, actually."

He picked up speed, cutting off a bright yellow Volkswagen Bug as he sped along the highway. Up ahead he encountered another slow driver, and, making an aggravated sound, reached up and flicked on the sirens.

The shrieking of the siren startled her and for some reason her fingers slid down to rub the scar on one of her wrists. She hadn't rubbed the scars since the first time she and Blake had made love, and the way she'd reverted back to the old habit left her unsettled. She touched the scars when she was nervous.

But why did she have to be nervous about? Officer Benson was taking her to a safe house; Blake had found the Rose Killer. There was no reason for the sudden sense of fear gnawing at her insides.

They drove for a while, sirens still blaring, and a good twenty minutes passed before Benson finally spoke again.

His tone jovial, he turned to her with a smile and said, "Want to know my take on cops?"

She furrowed her brow in puzzlement. "Um, sure, I guess."

"They're stupid."

Her head snapped up. "Pardon me?"

"You heard me. They're stupid." Paul Benson grinned. "All that training, the silly exercises at the academy—useless, in my opinion."

Her throat became tight, too tight to answer. And the hairs on the back of her neck tingled. Something wasn't right here. Oh, God. Something was most definitely *not* right.

She closed her eyes for a moment. No, nothing was wrong. Everything was fine. Benson was obviously just a little wacky.

"And the lack of instinct!" he continued, eyeing her with wonderment. "Someone calls you up, gives you a fancy detective title, and you say, 'Yes, sir, I'm on my way.' You tell them to roll around in the snow and squeal like a pig, and they'll do it. No questions."

Yes, sir, I'm on my way. Those had been Perkins's words. He'd said them on the phone when the senior detective had called...fancy detective title... *Oh, God.*

"Ah, so I knew I didn't marry an idiot," Benson said. He chuckled loudly. "Finally put it together, did you, Annie?"

I didn't *marry…?* Annie? Who was Annie? And why was he looking at her as if—

He chuckled again and every ghastly puzzle piece snapped into place.

She *knew* that chuckle.

She'd heard it before. Six months ago. In her bedroom. When a man had tied her to her own bed and carved into her skin and sliced her wrists with a knife so sharp she could still feel its blade and—

"Don't look at me like that," Benson chided. "You brought this on yourself, sweetheart."

Terror, thick and hot and raw, pummeled into her like merciless fists. With a strangled gasp, she fumbled with her seat belt, desperately trying to unbuckle it. She managed to snap it off just as a hand sliced through the air and connected with her cheek.

Pain stung at her skin. "Don't touch me!" She wanted to scream but the words came out in a squeak. She could barely breathe, couldn't think, but she forced herself to move. Her hand clawed at the door handle while the monster sitting beside her simply laughed again. They were speeding along the interstate but she didn't care. She would jump out and risk getting hit by another car—if it meant escaping this maniac.

She gripped the handle. Tugged. The door didn't open. Oh, God. Locked. It was locked.

Her fingers had just found the unlock button when she saw a flash of black steel in the corner of her eye. The butt of Benson's gun slammed into the side of her head.

White-hot pain sizzled her nerve endings. Her skull throbbed. Her vision became hazy and her pulse roared in her ears like the engine of a plane during takeoff. She fought the fog in her head, the blackness threatening to crash over her. No. No, no, no! She couldn't lose consciousness. Couldn't make herself vulnerable—

Another blow.

Harder this time.

God, it hurt. She blinked, forced her eyes to stay open but the damn things wouldn't comply. The strange, distant buzzing in her brain lulled her eyelids closed and she was floating away on a black cloud…sinking down…into nothingness.

Darkness.

Hell.

That was the last thought that found its way to the surface. She was in hell.

And then everything faded away.

Blake was on his way home when his cell phone rang. He saw Rick's number and quickly flipped the phone open. "What's up?"

"We might have a motive."

Excitement rose inside him. "I'm listening."

"Hodges was right. Grant's wife committed suicide. And, we tracked down her sister, who very candidly told us that Anne had been cheating on Francis Grant before she died. She apparently decided to end her life after her lover ran out on her."

"Are you one hundred percent sure Grant didn't do her in?" Blake asked warily.

"It's unlikely. He was out of town when she died, and according to the sister, Anne left a very long note addressed not to her husband but to her lover."

"Ouch."

"Hodges got access to Anne's medical records, and he also spoke with the family doctor." Rick paused, probably more for effect, Blake suspected. "The doc says Francis Grant has been on and off antidepressants for years now. Apparently he came home from Iraq suffering from depression and rage. Tried enrolling in the Chicago Police Academy but didn't pass the psychological exam. In fact, after Anne's death the doctor wrote Grant a prescription for more antidepressants. According to the pharmacy, it wasn't filled."

"Anything else?"

"A couple things actually. I just looked at a picture of Anne Grant. She bears an eerie resemblance to all our vics, Sam in particular. Oh, and the manager of Grant's flower shop mentioned that his boss owns a greenhouse."

Blake lifted a brow. "A greenhouse? Where?"

"Not sure yet. We haven't been able to find any more property under Grant's name. We're still looking, though. But apparently he uses the greenhouse to grow roses."

Blake's throat tightened with frustration. He liked everything he was hearing, liked how the pieces of this sick puzzle were slowly fitting together, but Rick was leaving out one very important thing.

"Where the hell *is* he then?" Blake snapped into the receiver.

"We still can't locate him. Apparently he dropped by the flower store yesterday and told the manager to mind the shop for a few days. Said he was going deer hunting."

"It's not open season," Blake muttered, an ill feeling creeping through him.

"I know." Rick's voice rang with a dark note of urgency. "Sounds like he's hunting for another victim."

"Or…" He suddenly felt physically ill. "He could be getting ready to come after Sam."

"That, too."

"So what the hell are we doing about all this?"

"The CPD is staking out Grant's brownstone and shop in case he shows up. I've been talking with some of the profilers, feeding them the new details and seeing if they have any ideas what this guy's next move might be. And the boys at the station are still trying to dig up the address of this greenhouse. There's a good chance he might be hiding out there."

Blake nodded. "Keep me posted. I'm on my way home to Sam."

"Don't leave her side, man."

"I won't."

He hung up the phone and stepped on the gas, his pulse accelerating as fast as the vehicle.

He'd been hunting this bastard for so many months that he'd almost given up hope. That the Rose Killer might have a name, a face, hands you could slap cuffs on, was enough to bring a triumphant grin to Blake's face.

He turned onto his street and steered toward the house. The second he pulled into the driveway, his entire body froze.

Something was wrong.

He hopped out of the SUV and examined his surroundings. He glanced at the unmarked cop car parked at the curb, but even the brief nod he received from Officer Daniels didn't ease his paranoia. He stared at the house. It looked like it always did. The front door was shut, the drapes over the window were closed, and yet his senses prickled with cold, shaky dread.

His gaze lowered to his feet and that's when he saw the footsteps in the snow. Two sets, both leading to the driveway. One was smaller, looked like a women's shoe, size seven maybe. Sam was a size seven. With urgent strides he hurried to the police car at the curb and tapped on the window.

"Who was here?" he demanded after Daniels rolled down the window.

The enormous bald man looked bewildered. "What? Nobody was here except the cop you sent over to pick up Miss Dawson."

An involuntary tremor crawled up his spine. "What are you talking about?"

"Detective Hodges called me and Perkins, said Miss Dawson was being taken to a safe house. Your orders."

His heart nearly jabbed through his rib cage and tore out of his chest. "Hodges was with me for the last hour. He didn't make that call."

"Are you sure?" Daniels's thick brows drew together in a frown. "We both got the call, and sure enough, an officer came to get Miss Dawson."

He felt sick. "When did they leave?"

"About an hour ago. Why? Did something happ—"

Blake bounded off without answering.

He climbed the porch and found the front door locked. Fumbling for his keys, he let himself into the house and deactivated the alarm. He called Sam's name. No answer. It wasn't that he didn't trust Daniels, but he'd had to see for himself.

His heart thumping in his chest, he pulled out his cell phone and was about to dial when he caught sight of the paper on the credenza. The note was written in a feminine scrawl. He snatched it up.

Blake, Officer Benson is here so I'll be quick. We need to talk when it's all over. Don't even think of avoiding me!

She'd signed her name simply as *S*.

Oh, Jesus. He didn't know who the hell this Benson was, but it was becoming sickeningly obvious that it wasn't a police officer who'd taken Sam away.

Nausea scraped at his intestines.

She was gone. The son of a bitch had been here, and now Sam was gone.

As sirens shrieked inside his head, Blake raced out the front door. He fumbled with his cell phone and violently punched in Rick's numbers. He must have stopped breathing at some point because when Rick finally answered the phone, Blake's lungs burned and his vision had blurred.

Gulping in oxygen, he gripped the phone so tightly he heard the sound of plastic cracking. "She's gone," he burst out. "He took her."

Rick sounded flabbergasted. "What?"

"Francis Grant, or whoever the hell he is. He took her, goddammit!"

"Are you sure?"

"She's gone, dammit!"

He wasn't sure exactly when he'd hung up the phone, or what he'd said to Rick before he did, but the next thing he knew he was in his SUV. Peeling out of the driveway and nearly skidding into a snowbank. He broke every traffic law on his way to the police station. Was he meeting Rick? Had they arranged to meet there? He had no freaking clue.

All he saw and heard and breathed was Sam. Terror lined his throat, his hands were shaking over the steering wheel, and whenever he swallowed, he tasted nothing but raw, clammy fear.

Blake slammed on the brakes when the police station came into view. The SUV slid two yards before it came to an abrupt stop, one tire over the curb.

When he stormed into the task force conference room, his partner wasn't there, but Superintendent Fantana and Burt Hodges were.

"Did Rick give you the details?" Blake barked, his voice sounding hollow to his own ears.

Fantana nodded gravely. "How long has she been missing?"

"Officer Daniels said the 'cop' came to the door about an

hour ago. The son of a bitch waltzed right up to the door and picked her up." Blake swallowed hard. "See if you can locate an officer named Benson. That's the name he used. He had a uniform, must have had a badge, too, because she—" his voice cracked "—she wouldn't have gone anywhere without being sure it was safe."

"I'm on it," Fantana said, already pulling out his walkie-talkie to get in touch with the dispatcher and track down Benson.

Blake stumbled backward, sagging against the cold wall behind him and forcing himself to regain his equilibrium. Dear God.

He needed to find her.

No, he needed to find her *alive.*

Because if he had to carry on his conscience the death of another woman he loved, he wasn't sure he'd ever survive.

The woman you love?

Even if he'd been in his right mind, that realization would have taken hours to examine, and he didn't have hours. Or minutes. Or seconds, for that matter.

The longer he stood uselessly in this police station, the longer Sam spent in the clutches of a maniac.

And the less chance he had of saving her before the bastard finished what he'd started and left her for dead.

Chapter 14

"Does he make you happy?"

The voice pulled Sam from her dreamless sleep. A quiet voice, but to her throbbing temples it sounded like a foghorn. As a searing pain sliced through her head, she whimpered and tried to lift one hand so she could rub away the ache. Her hands wouldn't move.

"Does he make you happy?"

Fighting back another sharp pain, Sam managed to crack open one eye. She blinked. Once. Twice. Three times. Hoped she was just imagining all this, that her mind had conjured it up for some sick reason or another.

No such luck.

As her vision focused and her head cleared, she knew she wasn't imagining a thing. She was lying on a small cot, her hands and feet were bound and the silhouette of a man loomed over her. Wherever she was, it was dark. Dark and cold, and it smelled like flowers.

Oh, God.

"Stop playing games, Anne, and answer the question," the voice said softly.

Sam tested the ropes binding her hands together. She tugged and twisted, but the knots stayed in place. She heard footsteps, and the silhouette moved closer, causing her pulse to quicken. No. *No.* Not again. This wouldn't happen to her again. She wouldn't let it.

As she lay on the cot fighting with the rope, the footsteps stopped and suddenly a humorless laugh filled the damp air. "It's no use. You're not going anywhere." Benson sounded annoyed. No, she had to remind herself. Not Benson.

By no means had she given up, but Sam knew there was no point struggling with the knots. She'd need to figure out another means of escape.

Blinking again, she turned her head and stared at the Rose Killer. A tiny window somewhere above her brought a gust of icy November wind into the room, along with a thin shaft of light that, as if on command, illuminated his face. He didn't look pleasant anymore, as he had in the car. Now his face was hard, his nondescript features twisted in anger.

The friendly "cop" from the car was gone. He'd become the monster from her nightmares. Flashing red eyes. That repulsive smirk she'd always imagined.

She stared at his face, wondering how this plain-looking man had become a crazed killer. Then she turned away, unable to look into those eyes a second longer.

"Don't turn away from me," he snapped. "And answer the damn question. Does he make you happy?"

"Does who make me happy?" she said hoarsely.

He sat on the edge of the cot. She tried not to cower. "Ted. Does he make you happy, Anne?"

God, who the hell was Anne?

Sam had read enough thrillers to know that stalling a killer usually worked about as well as dry glue, but she gave it a shot anyway. "Anne isn't here," she choked out. "But if she were, I'm sure she'd tell you that Ted didn't make her half as happy as you did." There. That sounded reasonable. Maybe he'd be placated by the words and let her go.

Fat chance.

His eyes darkened as he absently ran his fingers over shoulder. She shuddered.

"Then why did you slice your wrists?" he challenged, his white teeth gleaming in the darkness as he grinned at her.

It was obvious that he was disturbed, delusional, and Sam had no idea how to talk to him when he kept referring to her as another woman. When he looked at her with those tortured eyes and saw someone else.

But she had to try. The longer she kept him talking, the more time Blake would have to find her. And Blake *would* find her. She was absolutely sure of that.

Sam cleared her throat. "I don't know why she killed herself."

He slid his hand from her shoulder to her neck, and for one terrifying second she thought he would strangle her. He didn't, just touched her cheek so gently she almost threw up, and held her chin in place so that she couldn't look away.

"Twenty years, Anne. I gave you twenty years of love and marriage and friendship and companionship. And then you went out and screwed a man who didn't even care about you." His fingers tightened over her jaw. "I'll bet you feel foolish now, don't you, sweetheart? I'll bet you want my forgiveness."

Her throat was so tight she couldn't get any words out. Not that it mattered. This monster had obviously stopped listening to reason a long time ago.

"Well, it's too late. I won't forgive you, but I will—" he lifted his thin lips in a smile "—punish you."

Blake, where are you?

Fear paralyzed every muscle in her body, that strong front she'd tried holding on to slipping away as each agonizing second ticked by. She didn't want to be here. She didn't want to talk to this insane killer whose empty eyes scared her and tugged at her sympathy at the same time. She didn't want to go through this again. She didn't want any of this.

"I probably would never have found out about Ted, you know," he said pensively. "If the idiot hadn't decided to send you flowers from *my* shop, I would have never known what you were up to, Anne."

He rose, his too-big shirt rustling. She understood now why the uniform didn't fit him. It wasn't his.

Tears welled up in her eyes as she wondered if he'd killed a cop to get that uniform.

She watched as he headed for the door, praying that he was leaving. Maybe this was all he'd wanted, to talk to his dead wife for a bit, and now he was gallivanting off to do something else, like go bowling, or ice skating.

Right.

A strangled laugh tore out of her throat as she lay there, inhaling the scent of roses and staring at the doorway. She'd almost convinced herself that he'd left when he reappeared. He held a knife in his hands.

No. No, no, no! Her heart pounded violently against her rib cage. She flailed on the cot, blindly grabbing at the ropes on her hands while hot tears stung her eyes. She couldn't go through this again. She couldn't have this happen to her again. She *couldn't.*

In the large conference room, Blake turned to Hodges and snapped, "Have you managed to track down the address of that greenhouse yet?"

"No, but Samson is on it as we speak. I'll go see if she's made any headway."

Hodges left the room with hurried strides. When he returned a few minutes later, with Detective Carol Samson by his side, he wore a victorious expression. "We've got it," he announced.

Running her hand through her curly hair, Samson spoke. "The greenhouse was purchased under Grant's mother's name."

She recited the address and before she could get another word in, Blake took off.

"Blake, wait," Rick called after him. "What are you doing?"

"What do you think I'm doing? I'm going after her."

As he slid out the door, his partner scrambled to keep up with him. "You can't just charge in there."

"Like hell I can't."

Looking as if he wanted to shoot something—namely his partner—Rick grabbed his arm. "For God's sake, just wait a second. Let me talk to Fantana and then I'll go with you."

"I'll be in the car."

In the driver's seat of the SUV, he drummed his fingers against the steering wheel as adrenaline continued to pour through him in bucket loads. He didn't want to wait for Rick, didn't want to wait one more second when he knew Sam might not have that much time. But going in alone would be reckless, irresponsible. He couldn't risk making a mistake, because one wrong step could be the difference between Sam living and Sam dying.

"Fantana's team will follow us in an unmarked car," Rick said as he slid into the passenger seat. He held a sheet of paper in his hand. "Samson printed out a map for us. We won't be able to approach the greenhouse from the road. The area's too open. If he's near a window he'll spot us coming."

Blake pointed to another section on the map. "We can come in from the woods over here."

"The detectives will park down the road and we can radio for backup if we need it. Fantana's also arranging for the paramedics to be nearby, in case..." Rick never finished his sentence.

Blake's lips tightened. No, there would not be "in case." Sam was *not* going to be hurt.

He was about to say that when Rick's cell rang. Blake watched as his partner listened, then hung up.

"That was Fantana. They tracked down Paul Benson, the officer Grant was impersonating."

"And?"

Rick shook his head unhappily. "Dead in an alley off the Loop. Wearing nothing but his underwear. Fantana's put an ABP out on Benson's missing cruiser."

Rather than respond, Blake clenched his teeth so hard that his jaw ached from the pressure. Swallowing back his rage, he put the car into gear and sped away from the station. With the sirens on, he figured they could make the forty-five-minute drive in half the time.

"You're sleeping with her, aren't you?"

Rick's voice was quiet, but his words were so startling Blake's foot jerked on the gas pedal, pushing it down harder and causing the car to shoot forward.

"That isn't any of your business," he ground out, steadying the car's speed.

"It is if you plan on going all Rambo to save the swimsuit

model in your bed." Rick released a heavy breath. "Jesus, Blake. What were you thinking? You know better than to get involved with a witness. No, a *victim*."

His eyes flashed. "She's not a victim. She's a *woman*. And she's stronger than the both of us, you son of a bitch, so talk about her with respect."

Rick blanched. "Hey, hold up, man. I have nothing but the utmost respect for Samantha Dawson. Don't go twisting my words around."

He changed lanes without signaling, whizzing onto the highway ramp while avoiding his partner's shocked—and hurt—gaze. He didn't give a damn if Rick's feelings were hurt. *Sam* was the one hurting at the moment.

"I'm sorry," Rick finally burst out. "I'm sorry it sounded like I was lecturing or reprimanding you. I just want to make sure we're on the same page so we can rescue Samantha without any screwups, okay?"

Blake drew in a calming breath. Difficult, seeing as he was feeling anything but calm. Frantic, was more like it. And scared. So goddamn scared he couldn't even focus on the road in front of him.

"We're on the same page," he finally squeezed out. "I won't screw this up. I won't let what happened to Kate happen to Sam, all right?"

Rick looked shocked. "That wasn't what I was implying." He sighed. "What happened to Kate wasn't your fault. I was hoping you'd figured that out by now."

He didn't answer. He couldn't do this right now. Couldn't think about Kate and what took place in that warehouse a year ago. If he did, he would lose the last shred of control he had left, and at the moment, that control was barely a thread and it was ready to snap.

His silence ended the conversation and fortunately Rick didn't push it. The drive took them thirty minutes. The greenhouse was located north of the city, in an isolated area flanked by forest on one side, and near a stretch of farmland and a handful of industrial buildings, including a lumber mill that had been closed for years.

They left the SUV half a mile from their destination and entered the woods from the road. It couldn't have been five minutes before the trees cleared and the greenhouse came into view.

Though old and isolated, it was an amazing structure. The afternoon sun bounced off the enormous windows, the layer of dirt covering the glass sparkling under the light. The scent of flowers carried in the wind and wafted toward them, making Blake's nostrils burn. Sam was being held prisoner in there, at the mercy of a man whose reason and sanity had gone missing years ago.

His hand rested on his .38 and he slowly slid the weapon from its holster.

"I'll take the front," he said in a low voice. "You go around the back."

Rick nodded. His boots scarcely made a sound as he moved across the twigs and snow to the edge of the greenhouse.

Blake inhaled the chilly air. He found himself saying a silent prayer, something he hadn't done since he was a child.

Then he crept toward the glass structure, his fingers curled around the gun in his hand.

Sam gulped for air, desperately trying to swallow the debilitating horror glued to her throat. With a chuckle, the monster moved closer and closer, until he was kneeling down beside the cot.

"I'm sorry, Annie, but I have to make you pay." Regret flashed across his face. "I hate to do this."

"Then *don't*."

She batted at him with her bound hands but he easily avoided the useless blows and pushed her fists against her stomach with one hand. "Don't make this difficult," he hissed, his regret morphing into fury.

The red eyes. Oh, dear God, those red eyes.

She cried out as his other hand, the hand holding that gleaming knife, dipped lower and lower until it hovered inches from her collarbone. "I *loved* you." He dragged the blade over the collar of her cotton T-shirt. "But you betrayed me. They all betrayed me—the army said I wasn't needed anymore, cops kept me from being one of them— but your betrayal, Anne, yours was the worst, and now you'll have pay."

He sliced the top of her shirt with the tip of the knife. The seams hissed as they tore apart. He placed the cold steel against her trembling skin.

"So I have a present for you," he continued, those wild red eyes searing her. "Last time I tried to be generous. I only gave you one rose, in honor of the tattoo—you know how much I hated that tattoo, Annie?" His voice hardened. "This time I'm going to give you twenty-four roses, just like your lover did. But my roses will be the ones that last forever."

"Please." It was all she could choke out, but this man was beyond hearing her words.

"And this time, I'm going to sit here and watch you die." His jaw stiffened. "You won't survive this time, Annie. You won't be on the news and flaunt your adultery to all those reporters and screw yet another man who isn't your husband. Do you hear that, Anne? This time I'm going to kill you right."

"Let her go, Grant."

At first Sam thought she'd imagined Blake's voice, that she was so desperate to escape this sick scenario that she'd conjured up the voice of the man she'd prayed would save her. But when the knife froze over her chest, when the madman's head cocked in the direction of the door, she knew she wasn't hallucinating.

Blake. Here. A gun in his hand and his eyes so menacing, so determined and unwavering that she almost sobbed with relief.

She'd known he would come. That he'd save her. That she could trust him to protect her.

She'd known he couldn't walk away.

Blake took a cautious step into the small dark room, breathing in the scent of roses and mildew.

History repeating itself.

His eyes registered Sam on the metal cot, hands and feet bound, gorgeous face rigid with fear. His eyes saw Francis Grant, sitting at her side, knife in hand.

But his mind…his mind saw something entirely different.

A dark cavernous warehouse with high-beamed ceilings and exposed piping. A skinny man with a gun pointed at Kate Manning's back. Kate's green eyes, wide with horror, then flashing with agony as the gun went off. Kate jerking forward as she got hit. Kate falling. Kate dying.

Blake blinked. Forced his brain to focus on the present. He wasn't in the warehouse anymore. Sam wasn't Kate. And this time there would be no room for hesitation. Not when another woman he desperately loved needed him.

"You're under arrest, Grant. Drop the knife," he said calmly.

Francis Grant stumbled to his feet, his lifeless eyes widening with…recognition?

"You've got some nerve, showing your face here," Grant hissed out. "Haven't you done enough?"

Blake took another step forward. "Drop the knife."

Grant gave a humorless laugh. "Why? If I don't kill her, you will. Either way she'll die because of you, Ted."

In his six years on the Serial Squad, Blake had spoken to a lot of killers. Sane ones, crazy ones, delusional ones. Grant obviously fell under category number three.

"Your wife died ten months ago," he said quietly. "The woman in this room is not Anne."

Grant whirled around to look at Sam, then glanced back at Blake. "You're crazy. You think I don't recognize my own wife? You think the time I spent in the Gulf screwed me up that bad? You think the pills the doc gave me are messing with my head? Well, I've got news for you, Teddy. I never took a single pill. I didn't need to. I'm not crazy."

"Of course you're not crazy. You're grieving for your wife." Blake watched Sam from the corner of his eye. The ropes binding her to the cot looked strong. There was no way she would be able to undo those knots.

"I'm not grieving for her," Grant said with a firm shake of his head. "I'm punishing her."

With a bored look, the Rose Killer drifted toward the tall metal file cabinet leaning against the wall behind him.

"Don't move!" Blake ordered.

Grant ignored him. Set the knife on the top of the cabinet. Pulled open the top drawer.

"She has to pay for what she did," Grant mumbled, reaching into the drawer. "I won't let you interfere, Ted. I won't let you—" Without finishing his sentence Grant spun around with a small pistol in his hand.

"Drop it," Blake commanded. "If you don't, you won't get

out of here alive, Grant. So drop the gun, raise your hands and follow me outside into the squad car. Nobody needs to get hurt."

Grant's eyes flashed with blind fury. "She does," he snapped, jerking his head at Sam.

Blake's fingers hovered over the trigger of his weapon. He kept it aimed at Grant's heart. "This woman isn't your wife."

A feral look replaced the fury on Grant's face. He raised the weapon. "She needs to pay." He pointed the pistol at Sam. "She needs to pay for what she did—"

This time there was no hesitation.

Blake fired two shots into Francis Grant's chest.

With a strangled cry, the man stumbled forward. As he fell, he raised his gun and it went off, the deafening sound rocking the small room. Grant's wayward bullet connected with the ceiling, sending big chunks of stained plaster crashing down to the floor.

Adrenaline pumping through his veins, Blake bounded toward the man and kicked the weapon out of his hand. Grant's blood poured out of his chest like sticky cough syrup and stained Blake's fingers as he bent over the injured man.

"She needs to pay. She needs—" Grant gurgled, coughed out a spurt of blood, then gasped.

The man's dull eyes rolled to the top of his head.

Swallowing, Blake pressed his fingers to Grant's neck and checked for a pulse.

Nothing.

The Rose Killer was dead.

Heavy silence fell over the dark room, except for Blake's ragged breathing. Grant was dead. A wave of relief crashed over him, so violent that he nearly keeled over backward. It was over, finally over. Eight months of hunting, eight months of headaches and insomnia and—

"Blake?"

Sam's small voice sliced into him like a knife to the jugular.

With shaky legs, he hurried over to the cot and started untying the knots binding her wrists. He freed her hands, then her feet, then crushed her into his embrace.

"Are you okay?" he whispered into her hair, holding her so tight he feared he'd crack one of her ribs.

She clung to him, her tears wetting his shirt collar, her hands icy when she wrapped them around his neck. "I knew you'd come." Her voice was muffled as she pressed her face to his chest.

He planted a kiss on the top of her head before pulling back. "Did he hurt you?" he asked, sweeping his gaze over her.

Aside from the tears on her face, a purplish bruise at her temple and the red welts the ropes had left on her wrists, she looked uninjured.

She opened her mouth but Rick, Hodges and Samson burst into the room before she could speak.

"He's dead?" Rick asked in a brusque voice, kneeling beside Grant's motionless body.

"Yes," Blake said hoarsely.

Rick checked the man's pulse anyway, then glanced over his shoulder at Hodges. "Get the coroner in here. And tape off the scene. Forensics will need to do a sweep."

Still holding Sam, Blake got to his feet. "I'm getting her out of here."

"Blake, we need her statement—"

"Later," he cut in. "I'm getting her out of here."

He held her in his arms as if she were a fragile piece of china and carried her out of the room. Ignoring the cops streaming inside, he walked purposely out of the greenhouse.

Detective Carol Samson followed them, and much to

Blake's displeasure, started taking Sam's statement the second they stepped into the late-afternoon chill.

He set her on her feet, his arms cold and empty without Sam in them. He sucked in a lungful of oxygen and took a step to the side, turning to stare at the massive greenhouse behind them. How could a man who grew such beautiful flowers be so damn ugly on the inside? When he'd first entered the greenhouse, he'd been caught off guard by the beauty of the roses filling the space. He'd almost stopped— no pun intended—to smell the roses.

And then he'd heard Sam cry out.

He could still hear that note of terror in her voice, playing over and over again in his head like a bad sitcom rerun.

He took another shaky step back.

"Blake?" she said, noticing him edge away.

"I'm just going to speak to Rick," he replied roughly. "Go ahead and finish giving your statement to Detective Samson."

He moved away, but rather than heading inside to find Rick, he just stood on the icy path leading to the greenhouse and rubbed his temples. He watched as Sam softly recounted the events to Detective Samson.

His chest squeezed with relief. He'd almost lost her. God, he'd almost lost her.

"We're all done," Sam said in a quiet voice. She approached him from behind and wrapped her slender arms around his shoulders.

At the entrance of the greenhouse, the coroner's people were wheeling out the stretcher that contained Grant's body, covered with a black tarp.

Sam watched the scene, her expression unreadable. "I can't believe it's over," she murmured.

"It's not," he found himself choking out. "It's not over."

* * *

Sam lifted her head. What on earth was he talking about? Francis Grant was dead. The Rose Killer would never hurt another woman again, and it was all thanks to Blake Corwin.

Blake had rid the world of the evil that had lived inside Grant, but that wasn't the only thing he'd gotten rid of. In a couple of short weeks he'd succeeded in ridding Sam of the plague she'd lived with for six months: fear.

How could she ever repay him for making her feel alive again?

"Of course it's over," she said in a firm voice. "You killed him, Blake."

"That's not what I mean," he said gruffly.

She ignored her speeding heart rate. "Then what do you mean?"

"I lied to you, Sam."

She gulped, wanting so badly for him to continue but at the same time hoping he wouldn't. What if he finished the thought only to push her away again? Her heart told her that Blake couldn't be that cruel, but he'd been so adamant about ending their affair, so sure that she deserved something more than he could give, and she found herself falling prey to doubt and insecurity.

She finally found her voice. "You lied?"

"When I told you I wasn't whole. I didn't want to see it at the time but…I was wrong, Sam. When I'm with you, I *am* whole."

Her mouth went so dry it felt as if it were filled with cotton balls. Swallowing heavily, she met Blake's earnest gaze. "What are you saying?"

"I'm saying I want to be with you." He brushed his hand over her cheek, and she almost melted into a puddle on the cold ground. "I'm saying that I love you."

His words penetrated right through her clothing and heated her heart. "You love me?"

"I think I've loved you from the moment I met you. I love everything about you, Samantha. Your strength and your laughter and your scars and—" He broke off, took a long breath. "*Everything* about you."

Their eyes locked, and she nearly fell over backward. The emotion brimming in his whiskey-colored eyes made her weak.

"When I got home today and found you gone—" His voice cracked. "It was like someone tore my heart right out of my chest. The thought of losing you…" He drifted, the look in his eyes almost frantic.

He stroked her bottom lip with the pad of his thumb. "I know I acted like an irrational fool, but I promise you, Sam, I'm thinking clearly now. I'm always going to be stubborn and serious—I'll probably still be a demanding jerk from time to time—but I can promise you I'm not going to push you away again. I promise that I'll smile more often and I'll never play golf, and if you want to watch some Brad Pitt movies, I'll make the popcorn, okay?"

Laughter spilled out of her throat. "Those are some pretty hefty promises." Her chest suddenly clenched as she thought of something. "What about Kate?"

"Kate is gone," he said softly. "And it's time to let her go. She wouldn't want me to walk away from you." He gave a wry smile. "Actually, she'd be furious if she knew what I put you through."

"And the risks that come with your job?"

"You told me you could handle it." His probing gaze was filled with trepidation. "Did you mean that?"

She took a breath, nearly drowning in the pool of love reflected in his eyes. He looked so sexy standing there in front of her, his magnetic dark gaze awash with sincerity and his rough voice thick with emotion.

Could she handle the danger of his job? God, if it meant spending her life with this gorgeous, incredible man, she could handle just about anything.

"Yes, I meant it," she said firmly.

"Good." He paused for a beat. "Then I think that maybe we should get married. I don't think I can stand not waking up in your arms every morning."

Her head snapped up, but the surprise his comment evoked was quickly replaced by amusement. "Are you serious? That proposal was almost as bad as your snow angel."

He laughed. "I could get down on one knee if you'd like but the ground looks kind of cold."

She couldn't help but return the laugh. "How about kissing me, instead?"

His breath hitched. "Put me out of my misery first, sweetheart. Is that a yes?"

She took a step closer and twined her arms around his neck. "Yes." With a grin, she added, "You might be stubborn and demanding, but I love you, Blake. With all my heart."

And then she kissed him.

* * * * *

RICK'S APPOINTMENT with his attorney early Wednesday morning went only moderately better than his meeting with social services the day before. The prognosis wasn't great—but at least his attorney was going to file a motion for DNA testing. Just so Rick could petition to see the child…his sister's baby. The sister he didn't know he had until it was too late.

The rest of what his attorney said had been downhill from there.

Cell phone in hand before he'd even reached his Nitro, Rick punched in the speed dial number he'd programmed the day before.

Maybe foster parent Sue Bookman hadn't received his message. Or had lost his number. Maybe she didn't want to talk to him. At this point he didn't much care what she wanted.

"Hello?" She answered before the first ring was complete. And sounded breathless.

Young and breathless.

"Ms. Bookman?"

"Yes. This is Rick Kraynick, right?"

"Yes, ma'am."

"I recognized your number on caller ID," she said, her voice uneven, as though she was still engaged in whatever physical activity had her so breathless to begin with. "I'm sorry I didn't get back to you. I've been a little…distracted."

The words came in more disjointed spurts. Was she jogging?

"No problem," he said, when, in fact, he'd spent the better part of the night before watching his phone. And fretting. "Did I get you at a bad time?"

"No worse than usual," she said, adding, "Better than some. So, how can I help?"

God, if only this could be so easy. He'd ask. She'd help. And life could go well. At least for one little person in his family.

It would be a first.

"Mr. Kraynick?"

"Yes. Sorry. I was…are you sure there isn't a better time to call?"

"I'm bouncing a baby, Mr. Kraynick. It's what I do."

"Is it Carrie?" he asked quickly, his pulse racing.

"How do you know Carrie?" She sounded defensive, which wouldn't do him any good.

"I'm her uncle," he explained, "her mother's—Christy's—older brother, and I know you have her."

"I can neither confirm nor deny your allegations, Mr. Kraynick. Please call social services." She rattled off the number.

"Wait!" he said, unable to hide his urgency. "Please," he said more calmly. "Just hear me out."

"How did you find me?"

"A friend of Christy's."

"I'm sorry I can't help you, Mr. Kraynick," she said softly. "This conversation is over."

"I grew up in foster care," he said, as though that gave him some special privilege. Some insider's edge.

"Then you know you shouldn't be calling me at all."

"Yes… But Carrie is my niece," he said. "I need to see her. To know that she's okay."

"You'll have to go through social services to arrange that."

"I'm sure you know it's not as easy as it sounds. I'm a single man with no real ties and I've no intention of petitioning for custody. They aren't real eager to give me the time of day. I never even knew Carrie's mother. For all intents and purposes, our mother didn't raise either one of us. All I have going for me is half a set of genes. My lawyer's on it, but it could be weeks—months—before this is sorted out. Carrie could be adopted by then. Which would be fine, great for her, but then I'd have lost my chance. I don't want to take her. I won't hurt her. I just have to see her."

"I'm sorry, Mr. Kraynick, but…"

* * * * *

*Find out if Rick Kraynick will ever have a chance
to meet his niece.
Look for A DAUGHTER'S TRUST
by Tara Taylor Quinn,
available in September 2009.*

We'll be spotlighting a different series
every month throughout 2009
to celebrate our 60th anniversary.

Look for Harlequin® Superromance®
in September!

*Celebrate with
The Diamond Legacy
miniseries!*

Follow the stories of four cousins as they come to terms
with the complications of love and what it means to
be a family. Discover with them the sixty-year-old secret
that rocks not one but two families.

A DAUGHTER'S TRUST by *Tara Taylor Quinn*
September

FOR THE LOVE OF FAMILY by *Kathleen O'Brien*
October

LIKE FATHER, LIKE SON by *Karina Bliss*
November

A MOTHER'S SECRET by *Janice Kay Johnson*
December

Available wherever books are sold.

HSRBPA09

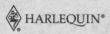

REQUEST YOUR FREE BOOKS!

2 FREE NOVELS PLUS 2 FREE GIFTS!

Silhouette® Romantic

SUSPENSE

Sparked by Danger, Fueled by Passion!

You're invited to join our Tell Harlequin Reader Panel!

By joining our new reader panel you will:

- Receive Harlequin® books—they are FREE and yours to keep with no obligation to purchase anything!
- Participate in fun online surveys
- Exchange opinions and ideas with women just like you
- Have a say in our new book ideas and help us publish the best in women's fiction

In addition, you will have a chance to win great prizes and receive special gifts! See Web site for details. Some conditions apply. Space is limited.

To join, visit us at
www.TellHarlequin.com.

Romantic

SUSPENSE

COMING NEXT MONTH

Available August 25, 2009

#1575 BECOMING A CAVANAUGH—Marie Ferrarella
Cavanaugh Justice
Embroiled in a strange case, recently discovered Cavanaugh and homicide detective Kyle O'Brien is assigned an attractive new partner. Transfer Jaren Rosetti has a pull on him he can't quite explain. But when the murders hit too close to home, Kyle will do anything to protect the woman he's come to need by his side.

#1576 5 MINUTES TO MARRIAGE—Carla Cassidy
Love in 60 Seconds
To keep Jack Cortland from losing custody of his sons to their grandfather, nanny Marisa Perez proposes a unique solution—a marriage of convenience. But while passion becomes undeniable between them, someone close is trying to destroy this family. And no one can be trusted when the threat becomes murder....

#1577 MERCENARY'S PROMISE—Sharron McClellan
Determined to save her kidnapped sister from Colombian militants, Bethany Darrow enlists the help of mercenary Xavier Moreno…with a little white lie. Xavier has a mission of his own, but when he discovers Bethany's deception, can he manage to trust this woman he's come to care for like no other?

#1578 HEIRESS UNDER FIRE—Jennifer Morey
All McQueen's Men
When Farren Gage inherits a fortune from her estranged mother, she also inherits trouble. She is threatened for money by terrorists who Elam Rhule has come to Turkey to kill, and the two are thrown together in close quarters, finding it impossible to resist the chemistry they share. She'll need Elam's help and protection, but will his heart be safe from her?

SRSCNMBPA0809